Also by Robin Stevens

Murder Is Bad Manners
Poison Is Not Polite

A WELLS & WONG MYSTERY

FIRST CLASS MURDER

ROBIN STEVENS

Simon & Schuster Books for Young Readers

New York   London   Toronto   Sydney   New Delhi

SIMON & SCHUSTER BOOKS FOR YOUNG READERS
An imprint of Simon & Schuster Children's Publishing Division
1230 Avenue of the Americas, New York, New York 10020

SIMON & SCHUSTER BOOKS FOR YOUNG READERS is a trademark of Simon & Schuster, Inc.
For information about special discounts for bulk purchases, please contact Simon & Schuster Special Sales at 1-866-506-1949 or business@simonandschuster.com.
The Simon & Schuster Speakers Bureau can bring authors to your live event. For more information or to book an event, contact the Simon & Schuster Speakers Bureau at 1-866-248-3049 or visit our website at www.simonspeakers.com.
Book design by Krista Vossen
The text for this book was set in Goudy Oldstyle Std.
Manufactured in the United States of America
0317 FFG
First Edition
2 4 6 8 10 9 7 5 3 1
Library of Congress Cataloging-in-Publication Data
Names: Stevens, Robin, 1988-, author.
Title: First class murder / Robin Stevens.
Description: First edition. | New York : Simon & Schuster Books for Young Readers, [2017] | Series: A Wells & Wong mystery | Summary: On holiday with Hazel's father, Daisy and Hazel secretly investigate a murder on the Orient Express, rushing to solve it before another murder occurs, or someone else finds the killer.
Identifiers: LCCN 2015050408| ISBN 9781481422185 (hardcover) | ISBN 9781481422208 (ebook)
Subjects: | CYAC: Mystery and detective stories. | Friendship—Fiction. | Murder—Fiction. | Orient Express (Express train)—Fiction. | Chinese—Europe—Fiction. | Europe—History—1918-1945—Fiction.
Classification: LCC PZ7.S84555 Fir 2017 | DDC [Fic]—dc23
LC record available at https://lccn.loc.gov/2015050408

For David.

You make me feel lucky.

First Class Murder

Being an account of
The Case of the Great Train Murder,
an investigation by the Wells & Wong
Detective Society.

Written by Hazel Wong
(Detective Society Vice President and
Secretary), age thirteen.

Begun Sunday, July 7, 1935

⎯⎯⎯ ⌾ The Orient Express ⌾ ⎯⎯⎯

FIRST-CLASS CALAIS-SIMPLON-ISTANBUL CARRIAGE:

Mr. William Daunt:
Owner of Daunt's Diet Pills

Mrs. Georgiana Daunt: Wife of Mr. Daunt

Sarah Sweet: Maid to Mrs. Daunt

Mr. Robert Strange:
Writer, brother of Mrs. Daunt

Madame Melinda Fox: Medium

Il Mysterioso: Magician

Countess Demidovskoy: Russian aristocrat

Alexander Arcady: Grandson of the Countess

Mrs. Helen Vitellius:
Wife of a copper magnate

Mr. Vincent Wong:
Director of Wong Banking, father of Hazel Wong

Hazel Wong: Secretary and vice president of
the Wells & Wong Detective Society

The Honorable Daisy Wells: President of the
Wells & Wong Detective Society

Mr. John Maxwell: Assistant to Mr. Wong

Hetty Lessing:
Maid to Daisy Wells and Hazel Wong

FIRST-CLASS CALAIS-ATHENS CARRIAGE:

Dr. Sandwich: Doctor

STAFF:

Jocelyn Buri: Conductor of the Calais-
Simplon-Istanbul Carriage

Part One
All Aboard for Murder

From the way my father is carrying on, anyone would think that the murder which has just taken place was our fault—or rather, that it was Daisy's.

Of course, this is not true in the least. First, holidaying on a train was *his* idea—and inviting Daisy too. And as for Daisy and me being detectives—why, it is just who we are. This murder would always have happened, whether Daisy and I had been here to detect it or not, so how can we be blamed for investigating it? If we did not, what sort of Detective Society would we be?

Naturally, murder is always rather dreadful, but all the same, after our last murder case (at Daisy's house, Fallingford, in the Easter holidays), when every suspect was someone we knew, this seems rather separate to us, and that is a relief. With one exception, everyone who might possibly have been involved in this crime was a perfect stranger to Daisy and me two days ago. So although we are sorry that one of them is dead (at least I am, and I hope Daisy is too), more importantly we are detectives on the case, with a puzzle to solve and a murderer to bring to justice. And we will succeed, whatever my father tries to do to stop us.

You see, although this murder does not seem as though it will be as upsetting for us as the cases of poor Miss Bell or awful Mr. Curtis, it may well be the most difficult to solve. Infuriating obstacles have been put in our way by grown-ups who want to ensure that the Detective Society is not able to detect at all. This is supposed to be for our own good—like eating vegetables and going for walks in January—but that, of course, is nonsense. Daisy says, Daisy-ishly, that they are simply jealous of our superior intellect. I know they are simply trying to keep us safe, but I wish they wouldn't. I am older than I was in April—and *much* older than I was last November—and I can decide for myself whether or not I want to be in danger. I am quite all right with being afraid for a while, if it means that we catch a murderer.

It is funny to think, though, that only a few days ago I was determined *not* to be a detective this holiday at all.

Robin Stevens

I do feel rather guilty about breaking my promise to my father. You see, when he found out about the murder at Easter, he telephoned to tell me that he would be coming to England in the summer holidays, to make sure I didn't get into any more trouble. I didn't really believe he would, but I was wrong. He really did come all the way from Hong Kong, by plane and train and boat. I ought to have known that when my father says he is going to do something, he does it.

On the last day of the summer term at Deepdean, where Daisy and I go to school, we were lazing on the lawn behind the dorm with Kitty, Beanie, and Lavinia, our dorm mates and fellow eighth-graders, cut grass scratching the backs of our knees. I had my eyes closed as I listened to Kitty and Daisy talk, the sun making the parting of my hair feel warm.

"And can you believe Miss Barnard chose *Elizabeth* as

Head Girl?" asked Kitty. Miss Barnard is our new head-mistress. She is surprisingly young for such an important grown-up, and most people are amazed when they first see her, but if you spend any time around her you can quite understand. Calm spreads from her like a cool wave—it only takes five minutes for her to make any problem vanish. She is my favorite of all the new teachers; I think she is slightly magic.

"And the new prefects too!" said Daisy. "They're all quite dreadful. Imagine, we shall have to be ruled by them for a whole year!"

"I know what you mean!" said Kitty. "You never know quite what they'll do next—"

She was stopped there by the noise of a car purring up the drive and parking outside the big front door of the dorm. We all sat up. Kitty's father was due at any moment, and we were expecting him, so my heart gave a little lurch when I saw a big black sedan with my father's secretary, Maxwell, at the wheel—and beside him, my father.

It was a very strange sight. You see, even though my father was the one who told me all about England when I was younger, so that it was all in my head before I ever arrived, and he is the reason why I go to Deepdean School, I had never been able to picture him in England before. He seems to belong to the Hong Kong side of my life. But seeing him there in his immaculate dark suit and tie, climbing out of the car to stand next to the front door of our dorm, was like holding up a stereoscope and watching the two halves of the picture come together with a snap.

My father is not tall, but he is determined-looking, with a square jaw and little round glasses that nearly hide his eyes—which he narrowed at me when he saw me sitting on the grass in such an unladylike way. I jumped to my feet, shamed.

"Goodness," exclaimed Beanie, eyes wide. "Is that your father? How funny—he looks exactly like you!"

"Beans," said Kitty, rolling her eyes, "who *else* would he look like?"

"I don't know!" said Beanie. "I mean—does *everyone* in Hong Kong look like you, Hazel?"

It was on the tip of my tongue to say that when I first came to England, everyone had seemed identical to me—but then I saw Kitty looking at me assessingly. "Awfully nice car," she said.

I blushed. "Is it?" I asked—although I knew perfectly well that it must be. My father always has the best of everything, wherever he goes, but explaining that to Kitty would be talking about money, and I have been in England long enough to know that talking about money is not nice, especially when you have quite a lot of it.

I curtseyed to my father, who was still watching us. Then the door opened and the maid ushered him inside. While he was speaking to Mrs. Strike (I rather dreaded that, in case she mentioned how untidy I have become—in Hong Kong I am absolutely neat, but I have discovered that to fit in here I must be careless with my possessions, and leave at least one thing on the floor every day), our trunks were brought outside. There was mine, with all its ship-dents and fading customs stickers—and there, next to it, was Daisy's.

That made it real. Daisy truly *was* spending the holidays with us! It was as though a great weight had been lifted off my shoulders.

You see, what happened at Easter—all the business with Mr. Curtis being murdered—meant that Daisy couldn't go home to Fallingford for the summer holidays this year. Her house has been locked up, and her family are all up in London for the trial. Daisy wanted to go too, desperately, but we were both absolutely banned by Inspector Priestley. Secretly, I was glad. I did not want to go at all. I did not even want to think about it—not that we have been able to get away with ignoring what happened.

The story of Mr. Curtis was all over Deepdean within a day of the beginning of the summer term. There were whispers up and down the corridors, and people turning and looking at us in Prayers. Daisy hated it. I could tell by the way she held her chin up and pressed her lips together. She does not like being pitied—it does not fit in with the myth of the glorious, perfect Daisy Wells. Of course, she

Robin Stevens

was very good about it, thanking everyone prettily for their concern when they asked if she was all right, but I could feel her burning up with rage next to me. The Marys, her devoted followers, bought her the largest box of chocolate creams I have ever seen and left them on her bed. When Daisy found them (luckily, I was the only one with her), she hurled them quite across the dorm. Then she picked them up, and shared them with the rest of us later.

To try to distract everyone, Daisy became more herself than ever, throwing herself into everything and being a Jolly Good Sport to show how all right she was. But beneath it all, she was not all right, and neither was I.

I hate thinking about Fallingford, and what happened there, and the trial that is about to take place, but as the term drew to a close and the day of its beginning grew closer, the words began to go round and round in my head: *The Trial, The Trial, The Trial.* My mind began to wander in lessons. My hand made restless doodles in the margins of my exercise books and my heart always beat a little faster than normal. Daisy clowned about just the way she always does, exasperating the teachers and delighting the shrimps and scoring five goals in the hockey match against St. Simmonds, but inside she was just as restless and unhappy as I was, and that was why I was so happy that we were both being taken away by my father.

The week before, he had sent me a letter about it:

Dear Hazel,

I hope you are well, and studying diligently. As agreed, I will arrive to collect you and Miss Wells on the morning of Saturday 6 July. I would appreciate you both being ready for a prompt departure—we have a train to catch.

I know that this term has been difficult for you and your friend, and I hope that this change of scene will be good for you both. I have been in contact with Miss Wells's parents, and they agree. It does seem to me that Miss Wells has a way of getting you into undesirable situations, and that you have a way of going along with her. I want you to try to influence her this holiday—you must be on your best behavior. I don't want any talk of crime. You have had far too much of that already. You will be discovering Europe, and enjoying yourselves—I want you to promise me that you will be a good, sensible girl, and show Daisy Wells how to be likewise.

Your loving Father

I was a little cross when he said that I follow Daisy. That is not true—or at least, not always. Nor was I sure that Daisy would enjoy being a good, sensible girl—but for my father's sake I decided that I would have to try. And he was right about us and crime, I thought. We had had far too much of that already. I didn't want to think about death and murder again.

I felt very virtuous as I decided that.

My father emerged, and beckoned us over. I rushed to meet him, and Daisy followed behind.

Robin Stevens

"Good morning, girls," he said, smiling, hands behind his back. Because of his schooling (he went to Eton), my father speaks perfect English.

I could tell that Daisy was surprised by this, although she did not show it. She only bobbed a curtsey and said, "Good morning, Mr. Wong. Thank you for letting me come with Hazel."

"I could hardly have left you with your housemistress all summer," said my father, who has very firm ideas about justice. "Anyway, every child ought to be shown Europe at least once in their life. It expands the mind."

He was not mentioning the other reason—The Trial—and I was glad.

"Now, I have a chaperone for you," he went on.

I froze. I remembered what had happened in the Easter holidays, with the governess Daisy's parents had hired. Surely not again . . .

"Not a governess," said my father, as though he had seen inside my mind. "Although I expect you to always be learning, I do not see why you cannot manage yourselves. However, I have obtained the services of a certain person you may recognize."

He waved at the car impatiently, and out of the back popped Hetty's frizzy red head, a new straw boater perched on it. She was beaming as she curtseyed. Daisy, remembering where she was, only smiled back regally, but inside

I think she was dancing with glee. My heart was leaping about too. If we were to be looked after by Hetty, that would not be bad at all. Hetty is the maid who works for Daisy's family at Fallingford, and she is a true brick—if she were not a grown-up, I am sure she would be an excellent Detective Society member.

"Now," said my father, shooting a slightly dark look at Daisy, "I want both of you to behave yourselves. Allowing you this freedom is a very great honor, and I expect you to earn it. Miss Lessing"—he meant Hetty—"will be your maid, and I expect you to be good and polite to her. Is that understood?"

"Yes, Father," I said.

"Now, into the car." He smiled again. "Trains will not wait, and we are catching the twelve fifty-five to Dover. Don't look like that, Hazel. The crossing will be quick." I blushed. My father really is good at knowing what I am thinking, and I had been dreading the ferry to France. Merely thinking about the big ship I travelled on from Hong Kong still gives me a churning feeling in my stomach.

"We'll be in France before you know it," he added. "And then the real excitement will begin!"

That was when Father told us exactly what our holiday would be. Daisy beamed, and even I had to smile. It was quite true. My father does not do anything by halves, and so a holiday around Europe could never mean less to him than the Orient Express.

III

As soon as we were on the train to Dover, Hetty and Daisy dropped their pretense. Hetty threw her arms around Daisy, laughing and kissing her cheek and saying, "Oh, I have missed you! It's been so strange, none of you in the house. Mrs. Doherty says to tell you that *she's* all right and that you're to remember to keep your strength up with lots of buns—I've got a tin of fudge to give you for the journey." Mrs. Doherty is the Wellses' housekeeper, a round and lovely person who makes the most delicious sweet things.

"I don't know much about . . . *you know*." Hetty wrinkled her nose so that her freckles wriggled. "I'm sorry, I've been kept out of things. I'm told I won't be needed until next month, so I can be with you now. Your brother wrote to us a few weeks ago, but . . . he's not right, poor Bertie, though he tries to hide it."

My stomach crunched, as it always did when I thought

about the courtroom, and the dock, and all the people I knew from Fallingford giving evidence at The Trial. Daisy, who had been happily munching the fudge, swallowed the rest of her piece in a lump, looking rather sick.

"Let's not talk about it," she said. "Can we?"

"I'm sorry, Daisy," said Hetty, taking her hand.

"Don't be." Daisy sounded rather fierce. "Just—we don't need to mention it, that's all."

Perhaps because of that conversation, the Channel crossing was even more miserable than I was expecting. Gulls echoed around the boat, and I could taste the sea when I swallowed. Maxwell and my father stayed in the cabin to write letters, but the three of us were sent up on deck to take the sea air. Daisy and Hetty stood at the rail, hands clapped to their hats against the wind, and ate buns, while I hung limply next to them, trying not to stare down into the swirling water or up at the swirling sky.

By the time we disembarked at Calais I felt turned inside and out, and the whole world seemed pale and churning. I cannot think how we got through Customs without my noticing, but we did—and suddenly we were in a train station, loud stone and steel and people rushing by, knocking against me. Station lights struck down through the clouds of steam from the trains and boiled them gold. The station pigeons sliced shadows through them with their flapping wings, and there was an enormous iron clock on the wall.

Robin Stevens

"Poor Hazel," I heard Hetty say, and Daisy added, "If she's ill again, that's five times, and I shall have won the bet." Although she, like me, had been on the train and the boat and through Customs, her hair was hardly disarranged, her dress was tidy and there was a soft pink color in her cheeks. I do think it is unfair, the way she manages to do that. And I had only been ill *three* times, whatever she said.

"Luckily, Hazel enjoys trains more than boats," said my father, hand on my shoulder.

I could hardly enjoy anything less, I thought as I was steered towards something long and large and covered in smoke. I blinked and the smoke cleared, and then I forgot all about being ill. All the colors came back into my eyes and the world slowed its spin.

There stood a great fat black engine with gold trim, panting steam. Behind it was a gleaming line of carriages, in cream and gold and blue, all emblazoned with the crest of the Compagnie Internationale des Wagons-Lits. Crates of glistening fruit and slabs of butter and bulging packets of meat were being handed up into them by porters in livery. Golden steps had been folded out of each of the carriages, and passengers in gorgeous traveling suits and hats that looked too large to fit through the doors were climbing up, chattering and waving to each other. For a moment it seemed as if all the wealthy people in Europe were there—and soon we would be among them. This was a holiday straight out of books.

The train was due to depart in just half an hour, and then the unhappy feelings I had been having all term, as though I were stuck in a dress two sizes too small, would be banished forever. We were about to rush across Europe on a headlong three-day journey—Paris, Lausanne, Simplon, Milan, Ljubljana, Zagreb, Belgrade, Sofia—and when we stopped again properly, we would be in Istanbul, a place so foreign that I could not even imagine it. I felt dizzy with gladness—or perhaps it was still the motion from the ferry. We were out of England, and away from The Trial, and everything would be all right. I was an ordinary not-quite-English girl on holiday with her father and her ordinary English friend. I smiled to myself. I could be on holiday. This was easy.

Our grand first-class sleeping car was at the very front of the train. It was sleek and newly painted in cream, with a brass plaque on its side that read CALAIS–SIMPLON–ISTANBUL. It seemed hardly real, but of course it was.

My father led us along the platform, his hand still on my shoulder; Maxwell strode along beside him carrying his briefcase. Hetty followed behind, balancing boxes and ordering the porter about—we seemed to have acquired a porter while I was not noticing things—and up to the golden steps that led into the train itself. We were about to step onto the Orient Express!

IV

B
ut as we approached the steps, someone pushed in front of my father, stopping us all in our tracks. "Excuse me," said my father, and the man turned round so quickly that he almost knocked into us. He was very large, wide as well as tall, and he had a moustache and a thick neck like a bull. He looked red and cross, and he squinted at us all as though we had inconvenienced him, just by being there.

"Excuse you," he growled to Maxwell. "You, sir! Move your servants!"

I felt my cheeks go red. The man had meant *us*, my father and me, although my father was wearing his best pinstriped suit, and I my new traveling coat with beautiful black frogging and pearl buttons.

My father's shoulders went back. He pushed his glasses up his nose and said, "Allow me to introduce myself. I am Mr. Vincent Wong, Director of Wong Banking, and this is my man, Maxwell. These children are my daughter, Hazel Wong, and her school friend, the Honorable Daisy Wells. And you are . . . ?"

"William Daunt," said the man. He did not apologize, or even look sorry. "Daunt's Diet Pills. My lovely wife and I are passengers on this train." He gestured, and a woman next to him, who I had hardly noticed before, stepped forward, clutching his hand.

I gasped. I could not help myself. It was not because of the woman herself. She was quite ordinary, small and pretty in a mousy English way, with pale brown hair, a rather soft, silly expression, and a smart powder-blue traveling suit and hat. But around her neck was the most glorious necklace I have ever seen in my life. I had never quite understood before the fascination people in books have about jewels. They are very sparkly, I suppose, but they don't *do* anything much. You can't read jewels, or eat them (I think if you could, they would taste delicious, like fizzy hot-house fruit). Seeing this necklace, though, I began to understand what grown-ups get so excited about. A string of diamonds lay like fire across the lady's neck—a trail of green and red and blue sparks that I wanted to put my hand against to see if they would feel cold or hot, and just at the dent of her throat sat the most enormous bright ruby, shining out so sharply that it made my teeth ache. Behind me Hetty gasped too, and Daisy said, "Now, *that* . . . !" She did not need to finish her sentence.

Robin Stevens

The woman's free hand fluttered up to her necklace. "How do you do?" she said in a silly little voice. "Isn't my William wonderful? He bought me this for our first wedding anniversary, so that I could wear it on this journey. It's simply *lovely*." Her fingers clutched her husband's sleeve, and she blinked up at him.

"Anything for my wife," said Mr. Daunt, and he patted her hand, beaming down at her fondly. "She is very precious to me. Now, if you will excuse us . . ." He pushed forward again, guiding Mrs. Daunt like a little child, and they went up the steps and onto the train together.

"Do you know who she was?" whispered Daisy. "Georgiana Strange!"

I must have looked puzzled, because she sighed and said, "She was absolutely the *wealthiest* available heiress after her mother died last year. It was such a scandal— her mother left her everything, and her brother was quite written out of the will. Simply every bachelor in England was chasing after her, but she chose that Mr. Daunt. He owns a factory—Daunt's Diet Pills, you know? I heard he wasn't doing well, but he must be now if he can afford to buy that necklace! Goodness, what a horrid man he is in person!"

"He can't be *so* bad," said Hetty, winking at us, "if he gives out jewels like that!"

"Hmm," said Daisy. "I suppose."

"Daunt's Diet Pills!" said my father, who had been speaking to the porter. "I must say, if their creator is anything to go by, they don't do anything for your character. I don't believe in diet pills, myself. Hazel, you must never take them. Now, shall we board the train?"

He held out his hand, and I took it and climbed up, out of the ordinary world, into the fat creamy body of the great, glorious Orient Express. All the noises from outside seemed to fade away at once. It was like being wrapped up and soothed in a beautiful blanket—the richest and most gorgeous imaginable.

The inside of the Orient·Express was like a palace in miniature, or the grandest grand hotel. The walls were rich, smooth, golden wood, picked out in beautiful floral marquetry; gold licked up the lamps and picture frames and doors. We stood on a soft, deep blue carpet that stretched away in front of us, down the glowing chandelier-lit corridor, and I knew that here I would have no trouble not being a detective. This was a place quite separate from the rest of the world, so full of marvels that even Daisy could not possibly become bored.

I looked down the corridor and breathed in its sweet, rich smell. There was a row of neat closed compartment doors along the left-hand side, and I wondered which ones would be ours.

A man with blond hair, a kind, bland, cheerful face and

Robin Stevens

beautiful gold buttons on his velvety blue jacket came bowing up to us.

"Mr. Wong, I presume?" he said, in a rolling, jolly accent. "And this must be Miss Wong and the Honorable Miss Wells. Welcome to the Simplon Orient Express! I am Jocelyn Buri, the conductor in charge of this sleeping car, and I will be looking after you on this journey. If you need anything—anything at all—you must only speak to me, and I will be delighted to be of service. My aim is to ensure that you are happy and comfortable. Now, let me show you to your accommodation."

"Are you French?" asked Daisy as he led us along the corridor.

"No, mademoiselle, I am from Austria," said Jocelyn, smiling at her. "The best country in the world."

"Oh," said Daisy, frowning to hear England dismissed like that.

We were in the most excellent luck. The front coach, which was taking passengers from Calais to Istanbul, had twelve compartments. Eight of them, the nicest, had one bed; the other four, which were supposed to be second best, each contained two bunks, one on top of the other. Daisy and I really ought to have had one compartment each, but as the carriage was quite full we had been placed together in a two-berth compartment—number ten, toward the front, up near the engine. Hetty was next door, in compartment eleven with the Daunts' maid, while my father was at quite the other end, in compartment three, which had a connecting door to Maxwell in compartment two. This is how my father prefers it—he is always having excellent business ideas at two o'clock in the morning, and bursting into Maxwell's room so that he can note them down. When I was younger and couldn't sleep, I would pad in to join them and curl up on my father's lap, lulled by the rumble of his voice all around me and the rise and fall of his chest under my cheek. Sometimes I would doze and wake up to find pieces of paper balanced on me, as though I were a writing table.

"Goodness," said Daisy, when our hatboxes and cases had been stowed in our compartment, and Hetty had tidied away our things in their neat little drawers, "isn't this marvellous? Like the best dorm imaginable. We can have midnight feasts every night if we like!"

"We could have them delivered to the compartment," I agreed.

"No!" said Daisy. "That would quite spoil everything. There's no point to a midnight feast that's legal. Now, to the important things. Did you know that this train is famous for being full of smugglers and jewel thieves? I read about a lady who was drugged while she slept, and in the morning all her jewels were gone. Do you think that will happen to Mrs. Daunt's necklace?"

Robin Stevens

"No!" I exclaimed, before I could stop myself. "Stop it, Daisy—just because there was a thief at Fallingford doesn't mean they're everywhere."

Daisy froze, the way she always does when I bring up The Trial, and I cringed a bit. I don't like reminding her—or myself—about it, but lately things have been coming into my head and out of my mouth before I can stop them.

"I—I only meant," I stammered, "that it isn't likely—"

"Honestly, Hazel, there can be more than one thief in the world. There are whole gangs of them, as you know perfectly well. And anyway, *that* wasn't only about jewels."

I could feel *that* sitting between us like a boulder. "I'm sorry," I said, and we both went to the door of our compartment to see who else was getting on the train.

V

The first person we saw was a small blond woman in a maid's uniform, pretty and pink-cheeked. She glared at us most crossly as she went rushing past. We could hear Mrs. Daunt's silly whining voice crying, "Sarah! Sarah! I need you!"

That must be Mrs. Daunt's maid, I thought, who was sharing with Hetty. She did not look very nice. The door to Mrs. Daunt's compartment closed, but through it we heard Sarah shout, "Well? What do you want this time?"

"William, she's being cruel again!" wailed Mrs. Daunt, just as loudly.

"Sarah, I've told you before, I won't have this!" snapped Mr. Daunt. He sounded positively furious. "Once more and I shall—" and then he lowered his voice and we heard nothing more.

Daisy looked at me, eyebrow raised. "Goodness!" she said. "How rude that maid was!"

"I'm sure it's nothing," I said, but I was worried. I knew that look. Daisy was having Thoughts, and Thoughts usually led to new cases for the Detective Society. I knew that Daisy wanted to take her mind off The Trial, and this was the easiest way she knew to do it.

I stared down the beautiful long hush of the corridor, blue and gold and glowing, and as I did so, the train shifted under me, shaking and growling like a living thing ready to leap forward. I wobbled and clutched Daisy's arm, and she grinned at me.

Then there was a commotion at the carriage door. Out on the platform, a sharp voice was shouting, "Come along! Come along, Alexander! Open the door, my good man!"

Jocelyn rushed forward and threw it open, bowing deeply. "Countess Demidovskoy!" we heard him say. "Master Arcady!" We craned forward, terribly excited, as onto the train came the person who had been speaking, with someone else following her. Bags and cases—a really surprising number of them—were piled on behind, and then the door slammed shut again, blocking out the platform noise like a blade coming down on a block.

The person who had shouted was an old lady—the little, bird-like sort that shrivels up rather than puffs out, with white hair and immaculately tailored gray traveling clothes. She clasped a thin silver cane in her gray-gloved hand, and her eyes darted about crossly. She was quite beautiful, and quite frightening.

With a lift of his finger, Jocelyn directed porters to collect the luggage—but while he was doing so the lady began to stalk down the corridor toward us. She was evidently not the sort of person who waited.

"My lady!" said Jocelyn. "May I introduce myself—?"

"There is no need to give me your name," snapped the lady—the Countess.

Countess sounded very European indeed; the sort of misty, dastardly European-ness of the villains in Daisy's spy stories. (Daisy, by the way, has been reading lots of spy novels this summer. Her favorite is John Buchan, and now she wants the Detective Society to have its own costume department. Daisy in a beard and plus fours would be pushing it a bit, I think, but Daisy says that this isn't what she means at all, and that I am just being obtuse. I wish Daisy would not use long words like that. Long words are *my* specialty, after all.) But where in Europe was this countess from? Her accent was very odd— it sounded like the girls at Deepdean when they pretend to be Russian spies. Could she be Russian? I knew all about the dreadful things the Russians had done to their royals, especially the Tsar and his family (Beanie had found out about the poor little princesses last term and wept for a whole day)—but I had never seen one in the flesh. I stared in fascination.

"I assume you will be attending us?" the old lady went on.

"Yes, my lady," said Jocelyn, bowing again. His cheeks had turned slightly pinker. "Now, we have you in compartment eight, and your grandson next to you, in number nine. His is a double, but its other berth is free. We hope you will both be quite comfortable."

Grandson? I thought. I pulled my eyes away from the Countess and looked at last at the person behind her. It was a boy who looked exactly the same age as Daisy and me. He was fair and thin-faced, with quite a lot of rather nice blond hair and good eyebrows; and he was clearly still growing, for his ankles and wrists stuck out awkwardly from his clothes, and his cheekbones were sharp. He looked like Little Lord Fauntleroy partly grown up. He caught my eye, and I looked away quickly. A boy!

"Humph!" said the Countess sharply. "That is not what I asked for. Two *single* compartments. This will be noted. However, I suppose you had better show them to me. Come along, Alexander."

"Yes, Grandmother," the boy said, and I blinked in surprise. The words were English, but the voice that spoke them was not Russian, and not English either. It was trying to imitate the clipped way that Daisy speaks, but there was a funny drawl behind the syllables that did not sound like any accent I had ever heard.

They came past us—the Countess ignoring us, the boy turning to stare at us. His look made me uncomfortable. It was direct and curious, as though he were used to looking at whatever he liked.

I did not enjoy it. I hoped that Daisy was thinking the same thing, and I was glad to see that she was staring back at the boy, coolly and without dropping her gaze. She stared in the same way as he did, as though she had every right to, and would do so whatever anyone else might think.

As Jocelyn passed us, he looked from us to Alexander, and winked. I felt myself turn scarlet. I do hate it when grown-ups imagine romance where there isn't any.

The doors to their compartments closed behind them, and then Daisy motioned me backward and our door swung to as well. She was looking quite gleeful.

"A Russian on the Orient Express!" she said, her eyes gleaming. "I wonder why she's here? Do you think she's fleeing a dark past? And why does that boy sound American instead of Russian? Ooh—perhaps he isn't really her grandson . . . Perhaps she's kidnapped him!"

"No she hasn't!" I said, realizing that Daisy was right about the boy's American accent. "He didn't look kidnapped at all." But Daisy was not listening to me.

"Hazel," she hissed, fizzing with excitement, "we are already discovering that this train is full of mysteries!"

"Don't, Daisy!" I said. "I told you, we mustn't do any detecting. My father won't allow it."

"I don't see what your father has to do with it," said Daisy. "If there's something going on, there's something going on, that's all. And if we're on the spot, we have to investigate."

"No we don't," I told her firmly. "Not this holiday."

I wanted to explain that my father wouldn't accept that sort of excuse. He wouldn't understand that we *had* to be detectives sometimes; everything, to my father, is a choice, and someone is always responsible for whatever happens. He is not happy until he can point his finger at them and make them put it right. I had not thought of this before, but I see now that that makes the two of us rather similar.

Daisy plopped down on the edge of her bunk and pulled out a hardback from her traveling bag. I should not have been surprised to see that it was *Murder on the Orient Express.*

"You can't read that, Daisy!" I said.

"Stop saying *can't.* Of course I can," said Daisy. "I can read whatever I like. And anyway, it might give us ideas for when we begin our investigation."

"There isn't going to be an investigation," I said.

"That's what *you* think," Daisy replied.

VI

The next minute there was a clatter of footsteps outside. Daisy dropped the book (she had only been
pretending to read it to annoy me, I knew) and
rushed over to our window, standing up on the bottom
bunk. She pulled at it and discovered, much to her annoy-
ance, that the windows on the Orient Express only drop
down a few inches. Still, she poked her nose out through
the gap. I clambered up beside her (as usual she had taken
the best view), pressed my face to the glass and stared as,
out of the shouting and the clanging and the smoke, a
gentleman appeared.

He looked like someone who *ought* to come out of smoke,
at night, with wolves howling. He had a huge black beard
and a peaked nose—and even a cloak with a red lining,
which swirled around him. He strode forward, a very determined look on his face, and there could be no doubt as to
where he was bound—our coach.

"It's Count Dracula!" I gasped.

"Hah," said Daisy. "Very good. But it isn't. It's *Il Mysterioso*. Goodness, fancy him being on our train!"

I must have looked confused, because she went on, "Don't you read at all, Hazel? He's in all the papers. He's an escape artist. Daring tricks. Astonishing feats. You know the sort of thing—like Houdini, only Italian, not American. Don't you remember hearing about him escaping from a packing crate at the bottom of the Danube three years ago?"

I shook my head. News like that does not tend to reach Hong Kong.

"Well, I suppose you wouldn't," said Daisy. "But he's really quite brilliant, although he hasn't done anything spectacular for ages. He's supposed to be planning his next trick at the moment. Everyone's on tenterhooks to find out what he'll do. Last time there were bears *and* a Tesla machine."

I still thought that Il Mysterioso looked rather a lot like a vampire, so it was with a thrill of excitement and fear that I realized he was climbing up the golden steps, his great black trunk lifted up behind him by the porters. Would he do a trick for us while we were on the train?

But now more figures had appeared behind him, and they looked ready to board our sleeping car as well. They could not have been more different from Il Mysterioso, or each other. One was a lady, very short and squat. She was black-haired and thick-jawed and her dress was all drapes and folds and panels of silky black, beaded and fringed. A dark tasseled scarf was wrapped about her shoulders too, and she wore black lace gloves—in fact, there was not a spot of color anywhere on her, apart from her lips, which were a deep heavy red.

The other was a man, skinny and unkempt. His hat was clapped onto his fair hair at an odd angle, his coat rather the worse for wear, and even his thin, aristocratic nose was slightly sideways. He and the lady both stepped forward at the same time, then stopped and glared at each other. He motioned her forward with a jabbing movement of his hand—as though he resented it—and the lady sniffed and went gliding forward without even acknowledging him.

Up she climbed, making the steps rattle, and up the man climbed behind her. Then they were in the corridor.

I heard Jocelyn greeting them all with great ceremony. Daisy jumped down from the window and motioned me across our tiny compartment (I marvelled again at how very pocket-sized everything was, like a grand hotel shrunk down almost to nothing), and we opened our door a little way and peered out again.

". . . and you will be in compartment six, Madame Melinda!" Jocelyn was saying. "I do hope you will find everything to your taste. And, Mr. Strange, you are alone in a two-berth compartment—number twelve—at the other end. Your sister, incidentally, is in compartment five, next to her husband, in four, and I'm sure—"

"My *sister?*" asked the thin man, Mr Strange. *Strange!* I thought. Hadn't Daisy said that Mrs. Daunt's name used to be Strange? "But—I—what do you mean, *my sister?*"

Jocelyn cleared his throat. "Is your sister not Mrs. Daunt? She and her husband are on this train, booked into this sleeping car. I assumed, since you were here as well . . . Did you not know?"

Mr. Strange, looking quite ill, clutched at his small case. "I—No, I did not know! If you'll excuse me, I need to go to my compartment—I must—"

But at that moment, with a bellow of bull-like rage, Mr. Daunt burst out of his compartment.

He slammed his door open, so hard that all of the crystal in the chandeliers clattered, and I actually felt his feet pounding across the carpet, rattling the floor even more than the starting engine. Her mouth an O of excitement, Daisy pushed our door open a little farther. I craned through too, squashed under her arm, and ended up with a view of people crammed together in great confusion.

"WHAT IS THIS?" Mr. Daunt was roaring. "YOU— BOTH OF YOU! I TOLD YOU TO LEAVE US ALONE!" He bumped into the wall and growled, "Curse these tight corridors!"

"Sir," said Jocelyn, and I heard a note of nervousness in his voice.

"Good evening, Mr. Daunt," said Madame Melinda—rather dramatically, I thought. She was speaking as though she knew him. "Yes, it is true. I will be traveling with you on this train."

"How—how DARE you? My wife and I are on HOLIDAY—can't you get your claws out of our lives for TWO WEEKS?"

"I received a communication from the spirit realm. They speak to me, and they told me that you would be here, and that it was most important that I accompany you. Georgiana is at a crucial stage in her progression. Under my guidance, she is beginning to truly communicate with her dear departed mother for the first time. Would you deny her the comfort she receives from our sessions together?"

"*Comfort!*" roared Mr. Daunt. "You're the one who's making her *un*comfortable—refusing to let her forget what happened!"

Mrs. Daunt's face appeared at the door to her compartment, and there was a gasp. "Madame Melinda!" she cried. "What are you doing here? You didn't tell me you would be on the train! And—and Robert! But . . . why are you here as well? I don't understand!"

Mr. Strange's face had gone very pale, with two little red dots at the tops of his cheeks. "I had no idea," he said.

"None! I am here doing research for my next novel. If I had known—after what your husband said to me the last time we met—I wouldn't knowingly come within a hundred miles of you."

"But that wasn't my fault!" wailed Mrs. Daunt, sounding more spoiled than ever.

"*Stop* trying to make Georgie give you her money," said Mr. Daunt. "It's too low of you. It isn't our fault you don't make enough from your awful pulp murder books!"

"Ladies," said Jocelyn, his face pink with worry. "Gentlemen. Please—the other passengers!"

"I want to go to my compartment at once," said Mr. Strange, in a trembling voice. "I won't be spoken to like this any more."

Jocelyn led him away, and with a growl of, "You haven't heard the end of this!" Mr. Daunt thumped back into his compartment. The door slammed behind him, but not before I heard the rising wail of Mrs. Daunt, exclaiming in distress.

"That man has the most unpleasant aura," said Madame Melinda. "It's no wonder he is not receptive to the spirits."

Il Mysterioso, who had been standing quite silently, taking everything in, made a vague noise in his throat.

Then he said, in a dark and rumbling voice, "I believe we are slightly acquainted, madame. You are Mrs. Fox, are you not? I recall your act, many years ago—"

"I am *Madame Melinda*, thank you very much. I am a medium of some repute, and only work with *private* clients. You must surely be thinking of someone else." But Madame Melinda sounded flustered, and I saw her tremble uncomfortably. I wondered whether Il Mysterioso had been mistaken at all. What sort of act did he mean? My ears had pricked up at the word *medium*. I knew that this was a person who contacted spirits, and that made me tingle with nerves. I do sometimes privately worry about the number of dead people I have come across. I know that ghosts are not real, but I am not sure whether *they* know that.

Two attendants approached Madame Melinda and Il Mysterioso, and they were shown to their compartments, with quite a bit of grumbling and rustling—the corridor was really very narrow, and both Il Mysterioso and Madame Melinda were quite large, either upwards or sideways. At last there was quiet again.

"*Well!*" said Daisy, in a stage whisper. "You can't say that there's nothing mysterious going on *now!*"

My head was whirling. Three more passengers in our sleeping car, and two of them knew the Daunts. Moreover, Mr. Daunt seemed to hate them both. Mr. Strange was a crime novelist, and Mrs. Daunt's brother. I thought about what I had just heard, and remembered what Daisy had said earlier: Mr. Strange hadn't been given any of their mother's money when she died, and he had never forgiven Mrs.

Daunt for it. Had he really not known that Mrs. Daunt would be on this train? Was it truly a coincidence? It seemed awfully unlikely.

Madame Melinda, too, was fascinating—a medium, who seemed to have been helping Mrs. Daunt contact her dead mother. It was clear that she and Mr. Daunt despised each other—Mr. Daunt seemed to have taken this holiday on the Orient Express in order to get Mrs. Daunt away from Madame Melinda. It had not worked out very well.

What would happen next? I wondered. How would everyone behave, confined in one train carriage, its corridor barely wide enough for two people to squeeze past each other, the little compartments only a few paces wide? The Orient Express was luxurious, but it was the very opposite of spacious, and it was warm in the summer heat. I imagined it as a pot, crammed full and ready to bubble over furiously.

Then I realized that I was thinking like a detective—and that, next to me, Daisy was bouncing with glee.

"Daisy!" I said, to quiet her.

"Oh, Hazel, you can't deny that what we heard was interesting. Arguments! Lies! Money! Death!"

"No it wasn't!" I said.

"You're just saying all this to stop yourself," said Daisy. "You're just as curious about this train as I am."

I flushed. This, like so much of what Daisy says, was

uncomfortably true. I had a horrid feeling that, like it or not, a new case was opening up in front of us.

I looked at my wristwatch and saw that it was three minutes to ten. In three minutes the Orient Express would pull out of Calais station and set off on its journey.

But then there was a flurry of movement outside on the platform. One more passenger was rushing toward the train, one hand clapped onto her wide-brimmed hat, under which glinted a sleek, short hairstyle. She wore the most beautiful pale pink traveling suit and coat set, and her silk stockings gleamed as she ran. Her face was perfectly made up, her heels were high, and her slender waist was belted most fashionably.

The last time I saw her she had looked quite different—nothing like the lovely, glamorous woman before me now. But all the same, I knew her at once—and so did Daisy.

It was Miss Livedon.

Robin Stevens

Part Two
The Spy, the Knife, and the Scream

I look back at what I have written so far, and see that all the important characters are there, lined up like actors at the beginning of the play. This is good, but Daisy is telling me to get on with it. I think she wants me to rush on to the murder—to the scream, and the locked door, and what we saw when it was broken down.

And I will, but there are two things that I need to mention on the way: the knife and the spy.

The spy came first.

The train was shuddering to life beneath us now, the rattles shaking their way up my bones. I leaned against the door and clenched my teeth, though of course Daisy remained standing, perfectly poised. Miss Livedon had to hurry up or be left behind. I heard Jocelyn call out something to her through the window, and then there was a rattle and a thud as the door opened. With a peal of laughter, Miss Livedon was inside. It was odd, because I had never heard her laugh before. When I knew her, she was entirely serious. But when I knew her . . .

I turned to look at Daisy. "It can't really be her!"

"It is," said Daisy. "We both knew it at once, didn't we? A detective should always trust her instincts."

"You're not . . . upset?" You see, the last time we saw Miss Livedon was at Fallingford.

"Of course I'm not upset," said Daisy, making a face as though I was an idiot—though I saw her hands clench against her skirt. "What would I have to be upset about? What I am is *curious*. What is Miss Livedon doing here? Does she know *we* are here? And does this have anything to do with . . ."

We looked at each other, and Daisy did not need to finish her sentence. Did her being here have anything to do with Fallingford? And how had she escaped being part of The Trial?

Footsteps were going past our compartment door. Daisy put her finger to her lips and we listened again.

"Such a pleasure," Jocelyn was saying. "*Such* a pleasure, Mrs. Vitellius. We had a letter from your husband entrusting you to our care—we hope you will enjoy your stay on the Orient Express. We have put you in compartment seven—I hope this will be to your liking?"

"Of course," said Miss Livedon, "I am sure it will. My husband will be most pleased. I'm afraid he's too busy to be

Robin Stevens

with me—copper magnates, you know, never a moment to themselves . . ."

The voices died away into the rattle and shake of the train, and we lost what else they said.

"Why is Miss Livedon calling herself *Mrs. Vitellius?*" I asked Daisy. "Is she undercover again?"

"Undoubtedly," she said. "And undoubtedly that husband of hers is entirely made up. She must be on another top-secret mission. Oh, isn't her life glamorous? Under the circumstances, I would say that there is only one thing we can do."

I looked expectantly at her, thinking how odd and difficult it would be to ignore Miss Livedon for the whole three-day train journey. If she was pretending to be someone called Mrs. Vitellius, she could not possibly acknowledge us. I suddenly wondered how we were to explain that to Hetty. She would recognize Miss Livedon too, of course, but she didn't know the truth about who she really was, and couldn't be told. Would she understand how important it was that we kept mum? Once again, I realized, intrigue was following us, plunging us into the most awkward situations.

"We must go to Miss Livedon's compartment immediately and confront her," said Daisy. "After all, we are practically colleagues. We've got detective badges, haven't we?"

We had—from Inspector Priestley, to thank us for our part in what happened at Fallingford. Daisy, I knew, had her badge in her neat little bag. Mine was still buried at the bottom of my tuck box, on a dusty shelf back at school. If you want to understand the difference between us, that is the perfect shorthand for it.

"We can't, Daisy," I said, horrified.

"Of course we can," said Daisy. "Come on, Watson, don't behave like a silly scared shrimp." And she marched out of the door.

The corridor swayed and rumbled as we moved along it. The train was really moving in earnest now, and out of the right-hand windows along the corridor I saw flashes of lights on stone buildings and cobbled streets.

I reminded myself that I must not detect—and the train, rocking beneath us, seemed to be chanting back at me, *must not, must not, must not*. It was so difficult to balance in time with the rocking of the train that I could barely concentrate on what was going on outside. Several times I had to steady myself against the marquetry flowers on the walls, and each time I felt guilty, pressing my hands against such lovely work. The crystal lights glowed above us, and at the other end of the corridor, past a row of closed compartment doors, sat Jocelyn, back at his post next to the compartment of Il Mysterioso, and the dining car; he was perched on a little chair with that day's *Paris-Soir* next to him. He nodded to us as we approached, and I suddenly felt uncomfortable—and not just because the train was

Robin Stevens

wobbling my insides. Although it had been wonderfully easy to listen in to the other passengers' conversations, we were always running into someone on this train as well. How could Daisy hope to creep about without attracting notice?

But Daisy, as always, rose to the occasion.

"*Bonjour*, Jocelyn," she said, in a very pretty accent. "*Excusez-moi*, but our tap appears to be leaking."

"Oh dear!" he said, jumping up. "I shall look at once." As soon as he had gone through our door, Daisy pounced. She leaped forward, placed both hands on the door of compartment seven and pushed hard. It swung open, and Miss Livedon was revealed, frozen in the act of stowing a hatbox in the luggage rack above her bunk. Daisy was inside before I could stop her—so of course I had to dart in afterwards, leaving the door gaping open.

For a moment it was very still and claustrophobic inside the compartment. Miss Livedon was gazing at us in utter astonishment.

"*Don't say anything,*" hissed Daisy. "*You heard us in the corridor and you opened your door and we came in to admire your things, all right?* Oh, what a lovely hat, Mrs. Vitellius! How simply spiffing!" She said that last part loudly, for the benefit of anyone outside.

Miss Livedon, to her great credit, did not even hesitate. She was an even better actress than I had thought.

"Oh yes," she said, just as loudly. "The latest Paris fashion. My husband does like to see me dressed up-to-the-minute. *What on earth are you doing here, girls?*"

"*We're on holiday,*" said Daisy accusingly. "*Hazel's father brought us. Didn't you know? What are you doing here, anyway? Why aren't you . . . in London? And why are you lying about your name again?* Golly, I wish *I* could have things like this. Oh, and what gorgeous perfume!"

Daisy could not bring herself to say, *Why aren't you at The Trial?*—but of course Miss Livedon understood.

"Isn't it? Chanel No. 5. *That, girls, is none of your business. As my name is Helen Vitellius and I have a very rich husband waiting for me in Istanbul, I have no reason to be anywhere else but here, and I'll thank you to remember that for the rest of the journey. I'm sure I have never met either of you before.*"

Daisy was not impressed by that at all. "*Hah! You want us to remember another invented name? I don't think we can manage that—not unless you explain what you're really doing here. Explain properly. Isn't that right, Hazel?*"

"Er," I said. "I do like your scarf."

Daisy rolled her eyes. Miss Livedon—Mrs. Vitellius—bother, I thought, how *was* I to keep up with all her names?—sighed.

"*If you say a word . . . Girls, this is serious. It isn't a game. If you tell, powerful people will be very cross with you. M will be very cross with you—you know perfectly well who I mean.*"

Robin Stevens

Daisy pursed her lips—we *did* know, very well—even though I still do not know exactly what secret things M does to make him so important. Daisy will never tell me. Sometimes I wonder whether *she* really knows.

"*Do you promise?*"

Daisy sighed, and then nodded at me. "*We promise*," we both said together.

"*All right,*" said Miss Livedon. "*I'm after a spy.*"

"No!" cried Daisy. "NOT Hermès!"

"*Yes, very amusing, Daisy. I have been given special dispensation not to appear in person at the trial. I am here because, according to the information I have been given by my contact, someone carrying secrets about Britain's military capabilities has boarded this train, and will be handing them over to German spies in Belgrade. Now, officially we're friends with Germany— but the government doesn't like the way Herr Hitler's been carrying on, and we don't want him to know any more about our operations than we can help. This spy has got past us too many times—been a thorn in our side for months. So here I am, to make sure that the spy—and the secrets they're carrying—never reach their destination. Whoever it is must be in this coach, and I mean to find out who they are. And if you know what's good for you, you'll keep your noses out of it, all right? It's serious, Daisy.*"

"Stop saying that! Why don't you tell Hazel to be serious?"

"*Because Hazel is always serious,*" said Miss Livedon, smiling at me. *"Now, girls, I know that you've done some detective work in the past, but this is different. This is international affairs, and you simply can't be a part of it. I've trusted you with the truth, and now I need you to absolutely stay out of it. No investigation, no daring missions—is that understood? It is so dreadfully inconvenient that you happen to be on this train as well."*

I felt rather apologetic—Miss Livedon was looking at us so fiercely. Daisy, though, was only cross.

"But—Miss Livedon!" she said. *"You can't tell us not to help! What if you need us for this investigation? You know we're good detectives, you remember what happened at Easter—it was us who solved the murder, not you!"*

"And this isn't a murder, Daisy. Argue all you like, but I won't change my mind—and if you do try to butt in, I will do all I can to prevent you. Is that understood?"

Daisy's pretty face was thunderous. Even I felt cross now. Here was *another* grown-up telling us not to be detectives on this holiday, and I found that I liked it less and less each time I heard it. We were being shut out of everything truly interesting.

Miss Livedon glared at us until we muttered, "Yes, Miss Livedon."

"Ah, but that's not my name any more, is it?"

"Yes, Mrs. Vitellius," we said obediently. Daisy said it through gritted teeth. "And you have lovely clothes," she added in a louder voice.

Robin Stevens

"*Top marks, Daisy. Remember, for as long as we are on this train together, my name is Helen Vitellius, and you met me five minutes ago. All right? And tell your maid—Hetty—the same.*" Jocelyn popped his head round the open compartment door.

"Miss Wells—Miss Wong?" he said. "I've looked at the tap, and it all seems quite in order now. I see you have met Mrs. Vitellius . . ."

"We were admiring her *spiffing* hats," said Daisy, beaming, as though she had not been having a furious row two minutes ago. "Come on, Hazel, I expect Mrs. Vitellius wants to unpack her pretty clothes."

Back we went to our compartment, and my heart was in my shoes. Mysteries wherever we turned, and we were not to be allowed to investigate any of them! It was not fair! I was trying so hard to be good, and to ignore the intrigue surrounding the Daunts—and then we were handed a real spy drama, under our very noses. I looked at Daisy and saw that she was fizzing with indignation too. Whether the grown-ups liked it or not, the Detective Society had discovered yet another mystery, and being told not to investigate it by Miss Livedon—no, Mrs. Vitellius!—had only made us more curious.

II

The train steamed on, rattling and ratcheting and groaning like a living thing. It was still making me feel rather ill—my whole head was filled with the noise, and my feet did not know what to do, with the floor shaking and bouncing up and down between every step. But then I sat down on the edge of Daisy's bunk (the bottom one) and stared out of the window, and saw the lit stone buildings of Calais sliding away behind us. It was like a night picture endlessly rolling away and renewing itself, just for me. The houses vanished and were replaced by cold silver fields; then there was a shining river, pale and slow; and then we rushed into a forest, and all I could see was the lit compartment behind me, and Daisy stalking up and down in her nightie.

It seemed to me that what we had heard from Mrs. Vitellius really could not be ignored. What was going on with the Daunts was strange, but there might be nothing more to it. A real spy, though, was simply too fascinating not to look into. Mrs. Vitellius might have tried to warn us off, but if we have learned anything from our two proper cases so far, it is that grown-ups are not always right. No matter what she said, we had to help discover the identity of the person selling secrets to Germany. If we did not, we would be letting down not only ourselves and our Detective Society, but the whole of Britain. I imagined the king looking sadly at me, the queen and the handsome princes behind him. I had to look after poor King George—he was very old, after all, and old people should not be upset.

Daisy was saying something, but I was so deep in my thoughts that I ignored her. My father expected me to be good this holiday, I knew that. But wasn't it better to unmask a spy who was working against Britain than to be *good*? Could he really object if we brought someone to justice?

I knew at the bottom of my heart that he could—but I did not want to admit it. My father would be furious at the way I was twisting the problem—but suddenly I felt that what he thought did not matter so very much. Yes, he wanted the best for me—but wasn't I old enough to begin to decide for myself what *the best for me* was? I am very nearly fourteen, after all, and people who are fourteen are practically grown-ups.

"Hazel!" said Daisy, jabbing me in the ribs, and I jumped. "I've been *talking* to you, Hazel. Listen up! You're dreaming.

As I was saying, we have found our mystery. Although *Mrs. Vitellius* has very good detective instincts, we know that she is not as successful as we are at testing her suspicions. We *must* investigate as well, and if you continue to go on about this being a holiday, as president of the Detective Society I shall have to order you—"

"You don't have to persuade me!" I said. "I've decided that I want to investigate this case as much as you do."

Daisy beamed at me. "Hazel, you brick!" she cried, and then she flung her arms about me so tightly that I struggled for breath.

III

On Sunday, I woke up to a glow of sunlight on my face, dreaming I was flying. The soaring settled into the rocking rhythm of the train, and I opened my eyes to see that the sun had risen behind our fringed scroll-down blind and was stretching across my white pillow. I breathed in the starchy smell of clean sheets and smiled.

And then I remembered: we were not just on holiday any more. We were beginning another investigation. I leaned out of my bunk and saw Daisy below me, splashing water across her face and humming.

"Hazel!" she cried when she saw me awake. "Get up! We've got a whole lovely day to be detectives in!"

We dressed, and out we went into the corridor. Jocelyn was at his post, yawning a little and smiling at us, and Daisy beamed back at him as we went past to breakfast.

"Allies," she said in an undertone as we sat at our table, "are always very useful. Remember that, Hazel."

We had decided that we would begin our investigations over breakfast, while we had all our suspects in the same place. The dining car looked lovely, all crisp white linen, sparkling glass, and deep fringed armchairs, but just like our sleeping carriage, it was a hotel dining room in miniature, everything so close together that we could hear nearly every word spoken.

The tables were set in twos and fours. Although only the Countess and Alexander were already having breakfast, it was clear that everyone from the Calais–Istanbul coach would be seated together at the end closest to our compartments. There were passengers from other coaches bound for other destinations at the far end, but we ignored them. They seemed to be citizens of quite another country, one that did not matter to us in the slightest.

Of course, my father and Maxwell and Daisy and I had been seated together. The Countess and Alexander (who smiled widely at me when I caught his eye; I looked away) were also at a table for four behind us—I wondered which passengers would be joining them. The table for two opposite us was still empty.

Then a white-coated waiter stopped by our table and put a telegram down on my father's plate. He unfolded it, the paper crackling thinly, and read it with a frown. My heart jumped hopefully. I knew that expression—it meant that there was business to be done. It seemed that my father

Robin Stevens

was just as bad at being on holiday as Daisy and I were.

"It's Bartlett and Evans," my father told Maxwell. "Their Oxford sale—it's going ahead. We must prepare the papers. Hazel, my dear, I had hoped to alight at some of the stations with you—Lausanne or Milan—today, but I'm afraid it won't be possible. I'll need to work on this for most of the day, so you and Daisy must look after yourselves. And tomorrow I'll show you Belgrade. Can you forgive me?"

I felt quite horrid. It could not have worked out more perfectly for me and Daisy—but of course I had to look disappointed. I do hate lying to my father.

I tried to distract myself with breakfast—which, luckily, was very easy. It was lovely. The waiters came round with steaming platters of sausages and eggs, like we had in England, but there were also plates of buttery toast and sweet pastries oozing with jam and chocolate—it really was just like eating cake.

Then Mrs. Vitellius came in, and the Daunts, Mrs. Daunt wearing that same glorious necklace we had seen the evening before. Behind me, someone dropped a fork, and I turned to see the little old Countess staring at Mrs. Daunt, her eyebrows raised in shock and anger, as though she had done something dreadful to offend her. I wondered what it might be. Mr. Daunt seemed in a much better mood than the night before: he pulled out his wife's chair for her before the waiter could reach it, and handed her her napkin most lovingly.

Mrs. Daunt, although she was wearing a very smart blue dress with her necklace, looked pinched and cross. "I'm sure I'm not well," she said. "I have the most dreadful headache. I wish you—"

"Dear Georgie, would you like coffee? Tea?" Mr. Daunt said over her. I was not surprised to hear that Mrs. Daunt had a headache—her husband was so loud and pushy that he must be exhausting.

"Coffee," said Mrs. Daunt. "Black."

Mr. Daunt shouted to the waiter, asking for coffee and eggs and fruit, and sausages for himself. Mrs. Daunt rested her head on her hands and winced. "I want Mama," she announced suddenly. "I want to speak to her. I've changed my mind—I'm going to ask Madame Melinda to let me speak to her."

"You are NOT—" bellowed Mr. Daunt. Then he took a deep breath and collected himself. "*Dear* Georgie, what have I told you? That woman's bad news—she's an absolute charlatan. She's only after one thing, and that's your money."

"I don't think that's true," said Mrs. Daunt, a rising whine in her voice. "That's just what you say. I want Mama! I want to speak to her!"

She really was like a first-year shrimp from school, I thought, all silly and sulky. But perhaps it was all an act. I knew from our previous cases that people could be very

Robin Stevens

good at acting a part. Despite appearances, could she be the spy that Mrs. Vitellius was here to catch?

I looked up and saw that Daisy was listening in as well, while pretending to admire the lovely fluted lamps on the wall behind the Daunts. I wondered what she was thinking.

Then I heard Alexander hiss, *"Grandmother!"*

I turned and saw that the Countess had got up from her table, taking absolutely no notice of him. Leaning elegantly on her cane, she tapped her way over to the Daunts, and then she stretched out a thin finger—in green lace gloves to go with her lovely green silk dress—to point it at Mrs. Daunt's throat. The ruby of Mrs. Daunt's necklace jumped like a heartbeat, and Mrs. Daunt herself shrank away into her chair, her face suddenly nervous.

"Morning," said Mr. Daunt, frowning up at her. "What can we do for you?"

The Countess's finger did not waver. "That ruby," she said sharply, "is mine."

Mr. Daunt was staring at her as though she had gone quite insane. The Countess, though, spoke slowly and clearly. "I tell you that you have my ruby, and I demand it back at once."

"Whatever are you talking about?" spluttered Mr. Daunt.

"That ruby," said the Countess, "has been in my family for five hundred years. However you came by it, it is mine, and one day it will be my grandson's."

"Are you a madwoman?" asked Mr. Daunt. "I bought this necklace fair and square for Georgie two months ago. The deed of sale and the insurance are in my luggage, if you'd care to look at them. I can even tell you how much it cost." I felt Daisy frown at that.

"You do not seem to understand," said the Countess, her voice sharp as metal. "When I left Russia, we were forced to sell it against our will. Now I have found it again, and it is time to get it back. It is not its price, it is what it means to our family. I demand that you return it to me, where it belongs."

"Pooh to that," replied Mr. Daunt. "Go away. I bought it, and I own it, and Georgie will wear it."

"How dare you!" cried the Countess. Her color was high, and her little bird-like chest was heaving. "You haven't heard the last of this—you'll see!"

And she jabbed her finger forward, so quickly that Mrs. Daunt squealed and raised her hands in front of her face. But all the Countess did was turn and stalk out of the dining car, her cane punching into the soft carpet as though it might bore holes straight through it. Alexander leaped up and rushed after her, casting one awkward glance over his shoulder.

Mrs. Daunt was gasping with shock.

"Eat your breakfast, my love," said her husband, patting her hand. "Don't worry about her. She's quite clearly a madwoman."

Robin Stevens

Mrs. Daunt pouted and her hand strayed to her throat unhappily. "It was awful, William . . ." she said. "Promise you won't let her take it?"

"Of course not," said Mr. Daunt, glaring around at us all as though he wanted us to forget what we had just seen.

But the incident still floated about the room, like a bad smell that would not go away.

By nudging my shin with the toe of her shoe, Daisy told me to hurry up and finish my breakfast, and as my father and Maxwell had begun a very serious grown-up discussion about people and places and numbers that all sounded much the same, it was easy for us to escape. Out of the dining car we went (I wrapped an extra pastry in my napkin and stuffed it into my skirt pocket, just in case), and found ourselves back in the corridor.

Jocelyn was still at his post. "Miss Wong!" he said. "Miss Wells! Do you need anything?"

"Oh, no," said Daisy, putting on her best being-nice-to-grown-ups face. "We only wanted to talk to you. The Orient Express is quite wonderful. Goodness, you must have the most exciting job. And so important!"

"Oh yes, miss," said Jocelyn, beaming. "I do enjoy it."

"Just think of all the people you must meet! Why, in this carriage alone . . . Is the Countess *really* Russian nobility?"

I could almost see Jocelyn thinking. It was not terribly good form, of course, to speak about the other passengers. But Daisy was gazing up at him, eyes wide, innocence shining out of her.

"Yes, miss," he said, and I bit my lip to stop myself smiling. He was under her spell. "I believe the family had to flee during the Revolution. She lives in England now, although the rest of her family moved on to America."

Five minutes later we had enough knowledge in our hands to write out a passenger manifest. Madame Melinda really was a medium, and Mr. Daunt's diet pills were doing terribly well now that he had married an heiress and invested her money in the business.

Mr. Strange, besides being Mrs. Daunt's brother, was a novelist—one who wrote gory, shocking crime mysteries. Their mother had disapproved of his books, and *that* was why she had left everything to Mrs. Daunt. Apparently he was on the Orient Express to gather information for his next novel. "Are they any good?" Daisy had asked Jocelyn, and he had replied, "Well, I shouldn't think your parents would like you to read them," and winked.

Alexander, although he lived in America, went to a most English boarding school—"Perhaps you know him?" asked Jocelyn.

I frowned. I did not like the way he expected us to make friends with Alexander, for all that he *seemed* all right. I wanted this holiday to be just Daisy and me, like old times.

We heard about Mrs. Vitellius too, and Il Mysterioso (though nothing new about either of them), and I really did almost feel guilty about tricking Jocelyn like this. He seemed such a thoroughly nice person—but detection is sometimes not a very nice thing.

Just then Mrs. Vitellius came out of her compartment, her beautiful deep-red day dress swishing elegantly about her.

"Good morning, Jocelyn," she said, and then she gave the two of us a very hard stare. I gulped. Had she guessed that we were disobeying her already by gathering information? It was strange to think that Mrs. Vitellius should suddenly be our adversary.

"Well, Jocelyn," said Daisy, without pausing at all, "thank you so much. Now come along, Hazel, we must go and freshen up in our compartment." She seized my arm and off we marched.

"Freshen up?" I asked, when our door had swung to.

"I had to say *something*, didn't I? Anyway, wasn't that a useful conversation? We've got some terribly juicy information. Hazel, before we go any further, I think you ought to write down a list of passengers, so we can see who our most likely suspects are in this case. As you know, we must be meticulous in our reasoning."

I wrote, and as I did so, I wondered. If Mrs. Vitellius

could create a new history for herself, who else might not be telling the truth about themselves? And which of them might have reason to betray England?

PASSENGER LIST

COMPARTMENT 1—Il Mysterioso, magician. He is not British, but he must travel often for shows. Why is he on this train? Is it significant that he is practicing a new magic trick? He must be watched.

COMPARTMENT 2—Mr. John Maxwell, secretary to Mr. Wong. He has not been in Britain since last summer, so he can be discounted.

COMPARTMENT 3—Mr. Vincent Wong. Our Detective Society vice president's father. As he has not been in Britain all year, it also seems impossible that he could be the spy.

COMPARTMENT 4—Mr. William Daunt, owner of Daunt's Diet Pills. We know that his business is doing well and he is very rich-he must be, to have bought that necklace-so he can't be spying for money. But could he have another reason? After all, he does not seem at all a nice man, and he must travel often for his business.

COMPARTMENT 5—Mrs. Georgiana Daunt, wife of Mr. Daunt. We know that she is a very rich heiress.

She seems quite useless, but is this just an act? Could she be the spy?

COMPARTMENT 6—Madame Melinda Fox, medium. She says she is here to help Mrs. Daunt contact her dead mother—against Mr. Daunt's wishes. But could this just be a cover?

COMPARTMENT 7—Mrs. Helen Vitellius, wife of Mr. Vitellius, copper magnate. Of course, this is an assumed name. She says that she is after the spy—and as we know that she is part of the British police force, it seems logical to believe her.

COMPARTMENT 8—The Countess Demidovskoy. She seems very angry about Mrs. Daunt's necklace—but is this just a blind? Although she lives in England, she is not British—might she be willing to sell British secrets to another country?

COMPARTMENT 9 (two berths)—Alexander Arcady, grandson of the Countess. American, though he goes to school in England. It seems unlikely that he would be able to travel unsupervised—he can really be discounted.

COMPARTMENT 10 (two berths)—Hazel Wong, secretary and vice president of the Detective Society. Daisy Wells, president of the Detective Society.

COMPARTMENT 11 (two berths)—Hetty Lessing, maid. A good egg.

Robin Stevens

Sarah Sweet, maid to Mrs. Daunt. We heard her being rude to her mistress!

COMPARTMENT 12 (two berths)—Mr. Robert Strange, crime writer. Brother of Mrs. Daunt. Left out of his mother's will. Says he did not know that his sister would be on the train, and he is here for research—is this true?

"You're quite right!" said Daisy, once I had finished. "If the spy is someone who travels often, the way Mrs. Vitellius said they were, then there are some people who are much better suspects than others. Il Mysterioso, for example, and Mr. Daunt. Of course, we don't know how much the Countess, Mrs. Daunt, and Madame Melinda travel, but we ought to be able to find that out. Sarah will travel with Mrs. Daunt, so Mrs. Daunt's answer will be the same as hers."

"And my father, Hetty, and Maxwell can be discounted," I said. "And Alexander."

"Mmm," said Daisy thoughtfully. "I wonder whether we can use him to find out information about the Countess."

"But we might not be able to trust him!" I said.

"I know," said Daisy, raising an eyebrow at me. "We can't trust *anyone*."

I realized that I was being foolish. After all, we had just deduced that Alexander could not be the spy. He was probably quite all right. It was just that we did not *know*. I did not like the idea of being friends with anyone we were not sure about.

"All right," said Daisy. "To action! The thing to do is this. We'll each follow half of our suspects. So you on Mr. Strange, the Countess, and Madame Melinda, and I'll keep on the Daunts and Il Mysterioso—and Sarah too. Remember, watch everything they do—and we must be especially vigilant at every station. That's where spies like to meet their contacts, and that's when they hand over the documents. If we're not watching we might miss the moment, and then the investigation will be ruined."

"What will we do if Mrs. Vitellius sees that we're watching? She'll be furious with us!" I thought someone ought to point this out.

"She may have set herself against us," said Daisy, "but, as we know perfectly well from our previous cases, grown-ups are not always very noticing people. Think of all the things we know about them, while they have no idea we're watching!"

Robin Stevens

fter that we set about uncovering Mrs. Vitellius's spy.

Now that I know what was about to happen I find it rather funny: we were so focused on the spy problem that we almost missed some very important clues to the coming murder.

We took up position in the corridor, staring out at the passing scenery and playing I Spy. This was not a chore— we had stopped in Paris and then traveled on through the French countryside during the night, and now we were rolling through high meadows which shone with summer flowers, while all around us mountains gleamed with dazzling snow. We saw chalets like brightly painted toys, dotted across the mountainside as though they had grown there, and when we forced the window open the little way it could go, the air was full of cowbells.

But we were also paying careful attention to what was

going on behind us. For quite a while the only person we saw was Sarah. She was kept busy, hurrying to and fro with medicinal preparations and hot towels and grapes from the kitchen. Her expression grew more and more cross, and once again I had the distinct feeling that she did not like her mistress or enjoy her job.

Once she took longer to return, and Mr. Daunt stuck his head out of Mrs. Daunt's compartment (which was next to his, with a connecting door). "Come along, Sarah!" he bellowed. "Don't keep my wife waiting!"

"Oh, William, I have the most dreadful headache," Mrs. Daunt whimpered from behind him.

"Poor Georgie," said Mr. Daunt lovingly, and ducked back inside. Sarah stalked past us and pushed open Mrs. Daunt's door again, and I heard Mr. Daunt snarl, "Idiot! Hurry up!" at her.

"Isn't he horrid!" I said to Daisy.

Then Mr. Strange emerged from his compartment. It was at the very end of the corridor, farthest away from the dining car, and so Daisy, who was facing that way, saw him first. I turned as I heard the sound of footsteps, and saw Mr. Strange striding toward us on his long thin legs, flexing his fingers and muttering to himself. He seemed very preoccupied—but then he saw us staring at him, and pulled up short. I wondered if authors were always so unkempt. He reminded me of a cat that has not been fed for a while.

In his right hand (spattered with blue ink, the nails quite stained) he held a cracked fountain pen. And then I saw that in his left was a small silver knife. It glittered villainously in the sunlight, and I gasped.

I feel a little foolish about the gasp, but really, a knife is not what you expect to see on a train with deep carpets and gleaming polished walls.

"What's wrong?" Mr. Strange asked, blinking at us. Daisy put out her hand to hold mine.

"You've got a knife," I said, rather stupidly—but I could not think of anything else to say. Spies carried weapons, I knew that—in Daisy's books they are always stabbing each other with knives hidden in gloves and hats and umbrellas—but they were not usually so obvious about it.

But Mr. Strange did not seem upset by my observation. "Oh, this?" he asked, wiggling it about between his fingers so that it flashed up brightly. "It's only a paper knife really. Use it for opening letters, and for inspiration. Friend bought it for me as a joke, you know? Crime writer—using a knife, you see?"

"Oh," I said politely. It did not look like something that was merely for opening letters. It was thin and wickedly sharp, and my eyes were drawn to it, as though it were giving off light, instead of merely reflecting it. I wondered what sort of inspiration it gave him. "Are all your books about crime?"

I had asked it simply for something to say—but Mr. Strange pounced on it like a cat on a bird and began to speak very fast.

"All books," he cried, "are about crime, because all life is crime. It is everywhere—it is unavoidable. Hidden passions! Dark secrets! Ah, the human heart hides many sins. I've put it all into my books—*Sands of Death* and *The Doom of the Stone*. They're good strong stuff—plenty of blood; it isn't my fault that the world isn't ready for the truths they contain."

"Golly," said Daisy. "How fascinating."

"The public won't buy them! Seems they only like their crime novelists to be ladies these days. A *man* doesn't cut it. Hah!"

I wondered if that were really true.

"But I'll show them," Mr. Strange went on. "I'm going to set my next book on a train just like this one."

"Golly," Daisy said again. "But hasn't that already been done by Mrs. Christie?"

"Imitation is the greatest form of flattery," said Mr. Strange. "Anyway, anything women can do I can do better. Don't know why I'm telling you all this . . . What do you know about murder? I expect you're still reading books about pixies."

I bit the inside of my cheek and tried very hard not to glare. Mr. Strange did not deserve any success at all, I thought. Daisy squeezed my fingers so hard that I winced. I could tell that she was in a blaze of indignation.

"Now, what are you standing here for?" Mr. Strange suddenly looked extremely fierce, and I would have stepped backward, only Daisy kept me beside her. She was not afraid, and I tried to be like her.

All at once Madame Melinda came bursting out of her compartment, black tassels flying—and then she saw what Mr. Strange had in his hands and staggered against the wall.

"Good heavens!" she gasped, her voice booming out. "He has a knife!"

Jocelyn, sitting at his post, looked up.

"It's a letter opener," Mr. Strange told her scornfully.

"A knife!" Madame Melinda repeated, waving her plump little hands in the air. The train rocked, and all the beads on her gown rattled like chattering teeth.

Jocelyn came quickly down the corridor. "Sir," he said, "if you would put the knife away—"

"It isn't a knife!" snapped Mr. Strange. "I don't see why I should do any such thing!"

"Sir," Jocelyn repeated, quite calmly, and at last Mr. Strange sighed and shoved it into the breast pocket of his jacket.

It was only then that I noticed that the Countess's door had opened, and she and Alexander were looking out, the Countess with a thoughtful look on her pinched face. Mr.

Daunt threw his wife's door open too, with Mrs. Daunt behind him, and even Sarah, back from the kitchens with a bottle and a glass tumbler, was watching excitedly. The corridor was very full, and at that moment the train seemed smaller and closer than ever.

So you see, that was the moment when everyone in the Calais–Istanbul coach discovered that Mr. Strange had a knife.

VI

ow we were nearly in Italy. At the border we
slowed and stopped, and the train dipped as
heavy men in black uniforms climbed aboard.
They were police, which was quite usual—my father had
explained to me that there would be police at almost every
border we crossed—but they seemed far more menacing
than the French police had been, or Inspector Priestley and
his officers back in England. They muttered to each other,
and then one of them pointed at me with the flat of his
gun, and said something I did not understand. Jocelyn said,
"*Lei è cinese,*" and the policeman frowned.

"Papers," he said. "Show me her papers. She is not from
Europe—what is she doing here?"

I seethed. I had as much right to be on the Orient Express
as anyone else.

But while I was only feeling cross, Daisy, as usual, was
noticing things. "Do you see how they're behaving?" she

asked me quietly, as the policemen muttered to Jocelyn and leafed through our passports. "They're worried about something. Their faces look nervous. See, they're pointing ahead, where we're going, and shaking their heads. Ooh, do you think they know about the spy?"

She said this quietly, which was good, because at that moment Il Mysterioso burst from his compartment (that was how he moved—in dramatic rushes, as though he were late for something exciting). He gave a start when he saw the policemen and their guns, which gleamed in the light from the chandeliers. I did not blame him for being shocked. They looked ugly and out of place, and I hated them. I believe he would have gone back into his compartment then, except that the policemen noticed him too. One of them grinned with excitement, and shouted, *"Il Mysterioso! A magic trick! Fai un trucco di magia!"*

Il Mysterioso gave a sort of fake grin, then put his hands to his lips, as though surprised—and when he pulled them away again a stream of red and blue and yellow silk came with them, a rainbow from his mouth. The policemen cheered.

The Countess's door opened, and Alexander looked out curiously. Then Il Mysterioso tapped his own door handle. *"Apra la porta,"* he said. "Open it!"

The policeman stepped forward eagerly and tried to open the door. The handle would not budge. It was locked.

Robin Stevens

Il Mysterioso motioned him aside and tapped the door handle again. He nodded at the policeman, who tried it— and this time the door opened, so easily that he nearly fell into the darkened compartment.

The policemen bellowed with laughter and clapped Il Mysterioso on the back. Alexander laughed too. I was impressed—but as I stared at Il Mysterioso, I was also confused. He was smiling, but the smile did not reach his eyes, and he flinched, just a little, from the policeman's hand. He seemed almost *afraid* of them. I wondered if I was imagining it—but when I looked at Daisy, I saw that she was thinking the same thing. Was this evidence? Did it point to him being the spy? I was not sure, but I tucked what we had seen away in my head to come back to later.

The policemen passed on to the next carriage and Il Mysterioso dodged back into his compartment. However, Alexander came out to speak to us. "Isn't he amazing?" He nodded at Il Mysterioso's closed door. "If I don't end up a Pinkerton, I think I'd like to be a magician."

Daisy blinked. "Pinkerton?" she asked.

"Oh, right," said Alexander. "Sorry. They're this American detective agency. I think they're incredible. My parents and Grandmother want me to join Father's business when I grow up, but I want to be a detective. I'm already practicing."

I did not know what to think. First, of course, it was

terribly un-English for Alexander to tell us about himself like this. I wondered if all Americans were so forward. And how odd that he should want to be a detective! Was this a good sign, or a bad one? I could tell that this bit of information had not impressed Daisy. She gets very protective about detection—in her mind, it belongs to us, and she does not like to see other people taking it over. "Huh," she said. "How lovely for you. Of course, Hazel and I have no interest in detection or magic at all. Girls don't, you know."

"Oh," said Alexander, his face falling for a moment. "I was going to say that I could lend you some crime books if you like."

"No, thank you," said Daisy freezingly. "We don't read—especially not detective novels."

This, from the girl who had packed an extra case full of novels, was so comical that I nearly spoiled everything by laughing.

"No, really?" said Alexander, looking surprised. "Why? You ought to. Read *Trent's Last Case*—it's ripping."

Daisy opened her mouth, but for once nothing came out. "Come along, Hazel," she snapped at last. "Let's go and talk about dresses." And off she swept toward our compartment, dragging me along behind her. I glanced back at Alexander apologetically. If he liked detection, perhaps he was someone worth being friends with after all.

But Daisy, unfortunately, had taken against him. "What

a bother!" she said once the door was closed. "That . . . that . . . silly boy has managed to stumble upon our best suspect."

"You really think Il Mysterioso is our best suspect?" I asked.

"Of course he is," said Daisy. "He's a suspicious character if ever I saw one. That beard—what if he's grown it to hide his identity? He's foreign and menacing, and that's what spies are like in all my books. And you saw the way he was with the policemen."

"But wouldn't it be better for a spy to look as though they fitted in?" I asked doubtfully, feeling a little pang that Daisy could believe that appearance was important. After all, the outside of me does not look the way heroes do in books. "The ones in books all get caught, so they can't be much good at it."

Daisy narrowed her eyes at me. I think she was trying to decide if I was making a joke at her expense—and perhaps I was, a little. After all, it has been a very long time since I believed in the myth of Daisy Wells. Yes, she is president of the Detective Society, but I am its vice president, and if I do not take her down a peg or two from time to time, who will?

"Anyway, he's the most likely spy. We must just carry on watching and hope that he reveals himself. And we must keep Alexander away from what we're doing. Really! Thinking he could be a detective!"

"But—why couldn't he be?" I asked. "If we can!" It simply came out of my mouth before I could stop it.

"Don't be an idiot, Hazel!" gasped Daisy.

"Sorry," I said. "I expect I'm wrong."

"I expect you *are*," said Daisy with feeling.

Through the walls of our cabin, we heard shouting. It sounded just like Mr. Daunt.

"Again!" said Daisy, raising an eyebrow at me. "Whatever's he upset about this time?"

"I suppose Sarah's done something," I said. But then there was a particularly loud shout, and I heard, ". . . WON'T ALLOW IT! SPIRITUAL NONSENSE!"

"Goodness!" said Daisy. "That sounds as though . . . He must really hate Madame Melinda being on the train."

I thought for a minute. Mr. Daunt seemed too preoccupied to have time for spying—but was this just a ruse?

"Wouldn't it be lovely if he was the spy?" asked Daisy, mirroring what I was thinking. "Or *she* was, and all that helplessness was just an act. Of course, it's unlikely, but a good detective never discounts anything. After all, you never know, do you? We must just wait and see."

VII

For the rest of that day we rushed through Europe in a
blaze of color and noise. I remember lakes and great
sweeping plains, and red-brick sprawls of Italian cities.
The train stopped in Milan for a while, and almost everyone piled out to stretch their legs. I saw Mr. Strange darting
among the iron fretwork of the station, muttering to himself
and scribbling things down on bits of paper, and Mr. Daunt
striding into a newsagent to buy the latest London paper.

My father sent Maxwell off with a pile of telegrams and
turned to me and Daisy. "Now," he said. "Business is over
for the time being, after all. May I take you on a city tour?"

Almost before I could nod, we were swept up into a taxi,
breathing petrol fumes and sour old leather, and a funny,
bright, spicy smell that I decided must be Milan itself. We
drove through little red-brick streets, bouncing along the
cobbles, my father drawing our attention to all the landmarks.
I felt most terribly excited as we swept past beautiful domes

and spires and great stone statues of people on horseback. There was a cathedral, its stone like filigree lace, and a market full of sweet good smells that made my stomach rumble with hunger. Then we turned a corner, and as my father pointed out La Scala (it did not look like much to me, but I suppose I still have lots to learn about culture), I caught sight of a tall, black-bearded, cloaked figure walking toward another man. As I watched, a parcel appeared from underneath the cloak and vanished into the other man's pocket—as quickly as a magic trick. Then the two men turned and walked away from each other as though it had never happened at all.

"Did you see—?" I gasped to Daisy.

"See what?" asked my father.

"That glorious façade," said Daisy smoothly—and I knew that she had seen everything I had. "Baroque, isn't it?"

So as far as we were concerned, the investigation was complete. We had found our spy.

After that, I only wanted to be back on the train again. It seemed an age before we were approaching the station—I was terrified that the Orient Express might leave without us—but at last, there we were, hurrying back along the platform where the train waited, gathering steam. Then the guards waved their flags, whistles shrilled and the train began to rock and tremble. It quite knocked me sideways again. I thought I should never get used to the way trains *moved*—like being inside something living, and breathing, and fierce.

There was a shout from outside, and Il Mysterioso came leaping aboard, cape swirling. I shrank back against the patterned wall, staring at him. His eyes looked wild, and I was terrified that he knew what we had seen. But then he nodded at us all (my father nodded back, and Daisy managed a weak smile) and strode past to his compartment. He evidently had no idea that we had been watching.

"What if he's already handed all the secrets over?" I whispered to Daisy. "Are we too late?"

"He can't have," said Daisy. "Mrs. Vitellius mentioned that the spy's main meeting point with the Germans would be Belgrade, didn't she? We'll just have to make sure we're ready, the moment we pull into the station there. Don't worry, Watson, we're still in time to stop him—now that we know it's him."

"But can we?" I asked.

"Undoubtedly," said Daisy firmly.

The train moved off, and after that the forests closed in and became something out of a fairy tale, dark and deep and turning blue in the distance. I thought I saw a bear, but Daisy did not believe me. "Really," she said, pressing her nose up against the window in delight, "this is quite the nicest place to have a mystery, isn't it?"

We stopped several times—in big city stations and

smaller country halts with just a strip of platform edging onto grass—and one of us always got out and loitered, peering down the length of the train, in case Il Mysterioso took the opportunity to do something else illegal. But we saw no more packages being traded. Indeed, he kept to his compartment. "He must be preparing the information to hand over in Belgrade," Daisy told me.

Mrs. Vitellius, though, seemed to be everywhere, passing up and down the corridor and striking up amusing conversations with the other passengers. "What a lovely brooch!" she cried, accosting the Countess.

"I had many brooches once," the Countess replied gloomily, leaning on her cane. "They are all gone. Taken. Stolen. I had earrings too. And bracelets, and necklaces—ah, if there was any justice in the world I would be back in Russia, able to chop off the heads of the people who took my necklaces. You know my necklace is on this train? This very train! Why, I would like to go and take it back. If I were in Russia, I should do it now."

"Oh!" said Mrs. Vitellius. "Really?"

"I intend to do so later," said the Countess, clenching her fists. "After dinner tonight. It is my right."

We tried to avoid Mrs. Vitellius, but of course it was terribly hard—and every time she saw us she gave us a quick, hard glance. It was turning out that having Mrs. Vitellius as an adversary was a most uncomfortable thing. Did she

Robin Stevens

know about Il Mysterioso? She seemed to be watching him as well—but then, she was watching everyone. Should we tell her what we knew: that he was the spy she was looking for? I felt we ought to—but then it would prove that we had disobeyed her, and I hated to think what she might do to us. She had been so dreadfully fierce the day before.

We watched and waited all afternoon, until I felt almost unbearable with it, breathless and excited like the day before Christmas. As we dressed for dinner, my fingers shook doing up the buttons on my dress, and I almost tore my collar. Daisy pulled her dress over her head, and it fell in gentle black and orange folds around her. Next to Daisy's lovely gown my own looked very silly and little-girlish. I blushed at its short skirt and polka-dots.

Daisy peered at herself in the gold-edged mirror above our basin. "Hmph. I'll do, I suppose."

"You look all right," I said shortly, standing on tiptoe to peep at myself over her shoulder. My hair was coming out of its plaits and I looked dreadfully pale.

"I wish I had your coloring," said Daisy as a bell rang sweetly out of the shuddering noise of the train, and a voice cried, *Premier service!*"

"Oh, goody, dinner."

There was a knock on our door, and when I opened it, there was my father, smiling at me.

"May I take you through to dinner, mesdemoiselles?" he asked, holding his arm out to me as though I were a grand lady. It was silly really, but I could not stop myself smiling back at him. I took his arm, and Daisy slipped her arm through my free one, and in a row (squeezing together slightly to get down the narrow, shaking corridor) we went into the dining car.

Our crisp white table had been set with ranks of glittering silver and crystal and glowing lamps, all shivering and dancing with the movement of the train. "Hazel, you are setting an excellent example to your friend," my father told me quietly as Daisy sat down and a white-jacketed waiter flicked her smooth white napkin out across her lap. "You see how improving this holiday has already been?"

"Yes, Father," I said, and sat down myself with a bump. The waiter poured out water (for us) and wine (for my father) without spilling a single drop. It was like a magic trick. I stared out of the window, past the soft reflected glow of the lamps on the tables, at the tall trees that almost hid the softening evening sky, covering and then revealing it again like moving fingers. Everything outside, beyond the pane of glass, somehow seemed very far away and unreal.

Another waiter came round with a steaming tureen of soup, pouring it out with a flourish right in front of my nose, and I clenched my spoon in my fist and took rattling, nervous sips. A speck landed on my collar at once, and I sighed.

Robin Stevens

The food was gorgeous, if rather grown up. After the soup there was chicken in a fancy tower, and then white fish in a creamy sauce—the waiters served it all from large silver platters; it was almost magical how they flourished it onto our plates without mishap. Pudding was crêpes Suzette—cooked at the table, and then set alight, so that shocking short bursts of blue flame flared across the carriage.

But I was almost distracted from the food altogether by what was happening all around it.

I was watching Il Mysterioso, of course. He seemed preoccupied, chewing away at his food automatically and quite ignoring the other people (Mr. Strange, Mrs. Vitellius and Madame Melinda) at his table. Halfway through the main course he took out a mechanical pencil and began to draw on his cloth napkin, tugging at his beard and muttering under his breath. Daisy nudged me and we both sat up straighter. Were these British plans being sketched out?

"Sir!" said the waiter. "May I fetch you a notepad?"

"No, no," said Il Mysterioso, waving him away. "This will do."

The Daunts had come into the dining car together. He seemed as loving as ever, but she looked even more sulky, flinching away from him as he guided her to her chair. She was still wearing the necklace, and it glowed mesmerizingly. I heard the Countess say, in a very loud stage whisper, "Look at our jewel!"

"Grandmother!" said Alexander. I glanced round and saw him blushing—and though I turned my head away quickly, I found myself thinking again that perhaps he was someone we ought to get to know.

Jocelyn made his way through the restaurant car on his way to the Calais–Athens coach beyond it, smiling and nodding to the passengers as he went.

"I tell you, my dear, put your mother out of your head!" said Mr. Daunt.

I suppose it came out louder than he had intended—and this was all the cue Madame Melinda needed. She stood up and glided over to the Daunts' table, the tassels and beads on her dress clicking as she did so. She really did glide—all her movements were very smooth and majestic, as though she had been oiled.

"Are you quite all right, dear Georgie?" she asked.

"Do go away," said Mr. Daunt. "Nothing to see here."

Mrs. Daunt pouted. "Oh, William!" she said. "Why *can't* I speak to her?"

"Indeed!" cried Madame Melinda, drawing herself up to her full height (which was not very high). "Georgie, my dear, do not despair. I have come to give you good news—I have received a Communication."

Mrs. Daunt's face suddenly glowed with hope. "From Mama?" she asked.

Robin Stevens

"But of course," said Madame Melinda. "She demands to be heard—tonight."

"Oh, do go away," said Mr. Daunt. "Haven't you been listening? I won't let you practice your mumbo-jumbo on my wife on this train."

"But, William!" said Mrs. Daunt. "I want to speak to Mama!"

"No!" shouted Mr. Daunt, his face very red. "This is for your own good! I want an end to this. There will be no more séances, if you please. You"—he pointed a thick finger at Madame Melinda—"shan't get any more of my money!"

With a sob of distress, Mrs. Daunt leaped up, necklace flashing hectically under the lamps, and rushed from the room.

"This is *your* fault," snarled Mr. Daunt, glaring at Madame Melinda. "I only want to make her happy!"

"Happy? She ran away from you! And I am not surprised. You have the most distressing aura. Quite red—almost black. I tell you, I will continue holding sessions with Georgiana until *she* asks me to stop."

"You dare!" roared Mr. Daunt. "You . . . you . . . get out of my way. I must go and look after my wife."

He strode out, growling to himself. The whole carriage sat, electrified. The only sounds were the clink and rattle of cutlery and the shake and roar of the train. Not one of us could think of a thing to say until Mr. Daunt returned a few minutes later.

"Wouldn't see me," he said, glaring across to where Madame Melinda had resumed her seat. He clearly meant that it was her fault once again. "Sarah! Go and see if she needs anything."

Sarah frowned up at him from where she was sitting with Hetty. "I'll go when I've finished," she said pertly, "Sir," and she went back to her crêpes. I was amazed all over again by her rude behavior, and surprised that Mr. Daunt did not tell her off. Instead, he ordered more crêpes, and the blue flame when they were lit threw his nasty red face and hairy moustache into sharp relief.

Mr. Strange was staring at him as well, I noticed; he had shrunk back into his seat as though trying not to be seen. He did not seem very sorry that his sister had been upset. On the contrary, he looked almost gleeful. I wondered if this was all just material for his research, or whether he liked seeing his sister suffer. I thought he did. He stood up and sloped out, and then Il Mysterioso got to his feet too. He looked so distracted that I wondered whether he had even noticed the argument. Was he too busy thinking about how he was going to hand over the secret information when we arrived in Belgrade? He left, and Daisy nudged me.

I knew we ought to leave as well, but just then the Countess got up, saying, "Now is the time to speak to her.

I feel it. No, Alexander, don't fuss! I'm perfectly all right. I can handle this family's affairs on my own!" She stalked past our table, hands clenched around her cane and lips set, and I knew that we could not go spying on Il Mysterioso while the Countess was in the corridor, bothering Mrs. Daunt about the necklace—because, of course, that was what she was about to do.

Daisy held up a hand with four fingers, and I nodded and waited—and then, just as the four minutes was up, Sarah stood up with a groan and a roll of her pretty eyes. "All right, then, I'm off to look in on Madam. Don't say I never do anything for you," she told Mr. Daunt as she passed by, poking him with her finger in a shockingly familiar way. He glared at her.

So again we had to wait—and then, as though there was a conspiracy to thwart us, up got Madame Melinda and Mrs. Vitellius. They went out together, Madame Melinda muttering crossly and glaring back over her shoulder at Mr. Daunt, while Mrs. Vitellius yawned and fiddled with her cigarette holder. Trying not to fidget, I swooped my spoon around my plate and wished it was polite to pick it up and lick it. There was still some syrup on it. But of course, my father would not think that civilized behavior at all. Daisy poked me. *Two minutes*, her fingers said.

And that was when we heard the scream.

VIII

It was such a loud, high scream that I think some people assumed it was the train's whistle going off unexpectedly. "Tunnel, is it?" asked Maxwell, startled.

But I knew it was a scream—and I knew it had come from a woman. The noise rocketed up my spine and made me sit up straight, as poised as Daisy. Who had screamed? Mrs. Vitellius? The Countess? Sarah? Madame Melinda? Or . . . *Mrs. Daunt.*

Daisy herself was out of her seat before any of the rest of us had even begun to move, rushing towards the sound. The worse something seems, the more Daisy needs to be close to it.

Mr. Daunt pushed past her and led the charge out of the dining car. Out we went into the corridor, which was already crammed full of people. Madame Melinda was beating on the door of Mrs Daunt's compartment—so it *was* Mrs. Daunt who had screamed—and shouting, "Georgiana!

Dear Georgiana!" Behind her was Mrs. Vitellius, having very believable hysterics, and the Countess, looking fierce. Mr. Strange stood frozen outside his room, an expression of terror on his face. Jocelyn came running toward us from the dining car, his wagon-lit cap falling off. There was no Il Mysterioso, though, I noticed. His door was closed. Where was he? How could he not have heard the commotion?

"OUT OF MY WAY!" bellowed Mr. Daunt, and he pushed Madame Melinda aside (or at least tried to—she is very solid, like a nesting doll, and so only swayed) and hammered on his wife's door. "Georgie!" he shouted. He dashed into his own compartment, and rattled the connecting door. "This is locked! GEORGIE! Why isn't she answering?"

He came barrelling back out into the corridor and bellowed this at Sarah, who was backed up against the wall, scowling.

"She wasn't answering earlier either," she said. "She's probably still sulking. She's got the key in the compartment with her." But for once she sounded more frightened than cross.

"I'm going to break down the door," announced Mr. Daunt. "GEORGIE!"

"Wait—sir—I can get a key!" said Jocelyn, still panting. "*Hang* your key," said Mr. Daunt. He backed up, cheeks red, white shirtfront gleaming in the light from the corridor's chandeliers, and then barrelled forward into the compartment door. It gave with a smash, and he staggered inside. Madame Melinda darted after him quite quickly, considering her size—and for a moment the doorway was quite obscured. Mrs. Vitellius was trying to get in, and the Countess, so I could not see—and then the Countess gave a cry and started backward, straight into me, at exactly the moment Mr. Daunt yelled, "GEORGIE!"

The Countess's face was crumpled up with horror. Madame Melinda let out a shriek, and Jocelyn, pushing past me (it was very rude, I thought—I only wanted to see what was going on), cried out too. "A doctor!" he shouted. "A doctor, quick!" and he reached up and pulled the emergency cord. The train let out a squeal, and then, with a grinding of brakes and a tremor that had us all falling against each other and shouting, the Orient Express began to slow. It shook and shuddered, and then at last, after what seemed like an age, it was still. In the eerie silence my ears still hummed with the ghost of the noise, and I felt myself trembling—it took me a moment to realize I must be shaking with shock, not from the train.

Daisy was up on tiptoe, trying to see over the crowd. Alexander was craning his head too, just as eager as she was— which was perhaps why Daisy—who, as I have mentioned before, truly hates to have any kind of competition—said, "Oh, bother *that*," seized my hand, and dragged us past everyone else into the doorway of Mrs. Daunt's compartment.

And I saw.

Robin Stevens

The compartment lamps were off, and the only light flowed in from the corridor. Half in the pool of it knelt Mr. Daunt, a heavy shape slumped in his arms. It was Mrs. Daunt—I could tell by her hair, and her lovely dress. But the hair, and the dress, and Mr. Daunt's white shirtfront were all now covered with bright blood; it was splashed everywhere, such an awful lot of it . . . And in the light I also saw the room key and Mr. Strange's knife, both smeared in blood as well.

My knees gave way, which was not very good detective behavior, but is the truth, and Daisy had to prop me up against her, squeezing my arm. She had gone very white and pink, her mouth open, and I could feel her heart beating through the soft fabric of her dress. She did not make a sound.

Madame Melinda had been struck dizzy too—she had staggered sideways to slump against the connecting door between Mrs. and Mr. Daunt's compartments, her scarf balled up in one of her fists. Her eyelids fluttered, and she said, "Georgie! Oh, Georgie!"

"If you're going to faint, go through to my compartment," growled Mr. Daunt. "Go on, open the door."

Madame Melinda rattled it. "It's locked," she said, fanning herself—and then repeated, "It's *locked*!" She pointed to the bolt with trembling fingers. Then she slid it back, pushing the door open. "Both this door and the main door—both locked, from the inside. Oh Lord! The spirits have been here, I tell you! The spirits! Nothing else could have got into this compartment!"

Quite a few people gasped. My brain swam. It was true. I had seen Mr. Daunt break the door down, and I had also seen Madame Melinda unlock the connecting door. But if they had both been locked from the inside, how had the murderer escaped? And how had they relocked the door behind them? Daisy and I exchanged a glance, and I knew we were thinking the same thing. Was this really a locked-room mystery, just like the ones we had read about in Daisy's books?

"WHAT IS GOING ON?" Mr. Daunt bellowed at Jocelyn.

"Sir," gasped Jocelyn, "I do not know—this is impossible. No master keys have been reported missing. I must ask my men, but I do not think—" Then he rushed away toward the dining car and the rest of the train, shouting, "Keys! Attendants! Show me your keys!"

Mrs. Vitellius wailed, and fainted very dramatically against the doorframe—and as she did so she pushed out with her hand, so I was knocked away from my vantage point. I should not have been surprised that Mrs. Vitellius did not want us investigating this either. She must think that it was the work of the spy.

But . . . was it? I wondered. Or was this something else entirely?

"Ow!" said Daisy, and I could tell that Mrs. Vitellius had shoved her as well. I looked up and caught them glaring at each other, just for a moment, and then Mrs. Vitellius was having hysterics again, and Daisy was busily wringing her hands and looking every inch the innocent girl caught up in a dreadful disaster.

My father said sharply, "Hazel! Daisy! Come *away* from there!"

He caught my wrist and dragged me backward—and although I knew I ought to be gathering clues, I was glad to be taken away from that horrid sight. I had a fierce moment of struggle with Daisy, and then she went limp, and allowed herself to be pulled away from the door as well.

Mr. Strange stepped into the space we had left, peered into the compartment, and then staggered backward, looking quite bleached with horror. "My knife!" he gasped. "But how . . . ? I had it before dinner, I swear I did!"

The Countess sniffed at him. I could tell that she was not the sort of person to be upset by murder after the initial shock. She blinked at the blood, and the body.

"Lord above," she said. "Where is the necklace? Where is my ruby?"

Jocelyn returned with a great jingling pile of wagon-lit master keys in his hand. "None are missing!" he said wonderingly. "None!"

IX

As well as the keys, he had a doctor—a passenger who happened to be traveling in the Calais–Athens coach, beyond the dining car. He looked very young to be a doctor, but he walked confidently with his chest puffed out. "I'm afraid there's nothing to be done," he said, bending down over the body and brushing Mrs. Daunt's hair away from her cheek.

"What do you know about it?" barked Mr. Daunt. "Where are you from?"

"Edinburgh, my good man," said the doctor, clearing his throat proudly. "Got my degree last year. Now I'm off to see the world."

"Scots!" said Mr. Daunt dismissively.

"Her throat has been cut," the doctor went on. "In these circumstances, there is very little I can do. All I can say is that the injury is recent—inflicted no more than half an hour ago."

"She has gone!" wailed Madame Melinda, who seemed to have recovered from her faint, and was back crowding up the corridor with the rest of us. "She has passed on, but she will return! Oh, I feel her spirit now, watching over us!"

Mr. Strange still looked sick. He hugged his arms about himself and groaned. "It can't be . . ." he muttered to himself. "It can't . . . I swear . . . that knife—it must have been stolen." He seemed upset—but more about the knife than about his sister.

My father was silent. I think he was in shock as well. You see, he loves his world to be controlled, and a murder quite ruined that. He looked somehow smaller as he leaned against the wall, and with amazement I realized that, for once, I was the expert and he was only an onlooker. It was a very strange feeling.

Mr. Daunt was shouting again. "I demand that you summon the police!" he cried hoarsely. "Someone has killed my wife! Where was the conductor? You! Why were you not at your post?"

"I—I was . . ." gasped Jocelyn. "Many apologies—I was with the conductor in the next carriage, discussing an important matter—"

"Disgraceful!" shouted Mr. Daunt. "Your negligence has caused my wife's death! If you had been here, the killer would not have been able to escape her compartment unnoticed! Your superiors will be hearing about this. And

I want everyone questioned! I want that charlatan woman to tell us where she was just now!" He pointed at Madame Melinda accusingly.

"How dare you!" she cried. "I was in my compartment! Mrs. Vitellius can vouch that she left me at the door only a moment before the crime."

Everyone looked at Mrs. Vitellius. She fluttered her hands. "Oh!" she said. "Yes, I suppose it's true. I heard her inside her compartment just before *the scream*."

Mr. Daunt looked furious. "Her brother, then! Where was *he*?"

Mr. Strange's mouth opened and shut like he was in a silent film. "I—" he said. "I . . . was in my compartment as well!"

"What nonsense! Why should we believe you?"

"It's true," said Mr. Strange, gulping. "Really . . ."

Wagon-lit attendants suddenly came rushing along our corridor in a confusion of blue and gold uniforms and moustaches.

"*Where* are the police?" shouted Mr. Daunt.

"Sir," said Jocelyn, for once quite without his usual calm air. "Sir, I beg to apologize, but there are no police currently on the train. We are in Jugo-Slavia. There are no police . . ."

Next to me there was a sharp intake of breath. I felt the pinch of fingers around my wrist. "Compartment," hissed Daisy. "Immediately!"

We began to edge away. "We're going to bed," I whispered to my father, and he nodded at me.

"Good girl," he murmured, and my stomach sank again.

I wondered what Daisy had realized. It must have been something very important for her to willingly leave the scene of the crime. I could tell from her jumpy movements that she was on the scent, but I could not think what it could be. I knew by now, though, that I could not blame myself for being unable to guess. What I have learned from our last two real cases is this: sometimes Daisy sees things that I do not, and sometimes I understand things that Daisy would never be able to. We are no better and no worse than each other. We are simply different.

"What *is* it?" I whispered as Daisy pulled me into the compartment and shoved the door closed, so that the sounds out in the corridor became hollow and through-the-wall. She ignored me, and began to rootle through the things that Hetty had so carefully tidied away.

"Something most important, Hazel! Something that proves . . . that this murder . . . was *planned.*" She puffed and muttered to herself, throwing aside comics and puzzle books and tins of secret emergency chocolate supplies.

"What do you think it means that the room was locked?" I whispered, not wanting to raise my voice in case someone heard us. "How could anyone have killed her and then escaped? Daisy, what if this is one of Il Mysterioso's tricks!"

"That is certainly a strong possibility, but listen to me first. We have just heard a most important clue: that the murder took place in *Jugo-Slavia*! Aha, here it is! View-halloo, Watson—*look*!"

Sometimes I think that Daisy's whole brain must look like a half-unravelled sweater, everything barely holding together but connected to everything else. What she held up was the book she had been reading earlier that day, its title blazed across the front: *Murder on the Orient Express*.

"Daisy," I said. "For the hundredth time, we aren't in a book."

"Hazel, you *must* stop reading the classics and embrace proper fiction. If you had bothered to read this book, as I have been asking you to for months, you would know that in it the victim is stabbed, at night, in his compartment. And *where* is he stabbed?"

"In the heart?" I guessed.

"*In Jugo-Slavia*. Where there are no police on the train! You saw how the Italian police got on when we crossed the border? Well, they do that in every country except Jugo-Slavia. I don't think the police here are very good. Anyway, it's a fact. And it's a fact that anyone who's read *Murder on the Orient Express* will know. That makes Jugo-Slavia the perfect place on the train line to commit a crime. Now, it is simply *too much* to say that a real-life stabbing on the Orient Express, in Jugo-Slavia, a year after Mrs. Christie wrote her book, is simply a coincidence. Which means that it isn't. The person who killed Mrs. Daunt has read this book, just like me. They knew that this would be the best place on the line to murder her. Which means that this was *planned*. This was not a spur-of-the-moment murder at all. Add to that the locked room and the stolen knife—if it *was* stolen . . ." Daisy's eyes lit up. "Oh, Hazel, we are up against an extremely cunning murderer—a worthy opponent for our third case! I have the feeling that this may be the Detective Society's most exciting adventure yet!"

X

In her enthusiasm, Daisy had been speaking quite loudly—and she had not quite closed the door after all. A moment later, and we would regret both things terribly.

Our compartment door opened properly, and there, framed in the doorway, was Mrs. Vitellius. Her face was set and cross—I realized that she must have heard every word. She knew that we intended to carry on detecting, despite what she had said to us. I was frozen, horror-struck, and even Daisy's, "Oh, hello, Mrs. Vitellius. Are you quite all right?" sounded rather thin and wobbly.

Mrs. Vitellius narrowed her eyes at us, and then she staggered backward, fanning herself and crying, "*Oh!*"

That, of course, got the attention of my father, and a moment later he was by her side. He still had the dazed, lost look I had seen in his eyes earlier, and I knew at once that Mrs. Vitellius would be able to make him believe anything she liked.

"Are you quite well, Mrs. Vitellius?" he asked.

"Oh," she said, fluttering, "why, I was just passing the girls' compartment, and I heard them saying the most dreadful things about poor Mrs. Daunt. Why, it sounded as though . . . they were pretending that they were going to be detectives and solve her murder!"

I hardly dared look up at my father—but then I did, and saw that his lips had gone very, very thin. That, I knew, was a very, very bad sign.

"Mrs. Vitellius, many apologies if the girls have upset you. I shall deal with this. Hazel Wong," he said coldly. "Up. Miss Wells, please leave the room. Now."

"Oh, can't I—" Daisy began, but my father merely said, "Out of the room, Miss Wells, if you please."

Daisy slunk out, the closest to cowed I have ever seen her, and the door closed after her. Inwardly, I was shrivelling up like a piece of burning paper.

I glanced up at my father and he glared at me through his little round glasses. I could tell that whatever was coming would be very serious indeed. And so it was.

"Hazel Wong, I have spoken to you about this before. You gave me your word that you would behave yourself on this holiday, and show Miss Wells how to behave as well—behave the way schoolgirls should. And that means no playing games with serious crimes."

"But—" I began, before I could stop myself.

"Quiet!" said my father. "Hazel, I don't like what has happened to you this year. I don't like the way Miss Wells seems to be always dragging you into danger, instead of keeping you out of it."

I wanted to protest that it was me dragging Daisy into danger just as much as the other way round—but I knew when to keep silent.

"Hazel, you are an extremely clever young lady, but crime—murder—is a dangerous, grown-up thing. It does not concern you, and I do not want you concerning yourself with it. What has happened to Mrs. Daunt must be dealt with, but it is not up to either of you to do so. Now, until this business is cleared up I want absolute goodness and quiet. I shall ask Hetty to keep a much closer eye on you, and I shall be watching you as well. I cannot have you putting yourselves in danger. Is that clear? Hazel, it is all very well you being clever, but you can't be clever if you're dead. Do you understand?"

"Yes, Father," I said, my heart pounding. Crossness and shame and fear were all tangled up inside me, so that I could not tell which of them I really felt. But I did know, suddenly, that for once my father was not right. We were not playing at being detectives, we *were* detectives, and it was up to us to investigate the crime and put things right. Once again there was a murderer to bring to justice.

That thought made me feel very odd. I am used to listening absolutely to my father. I have always thought he is the wisest person I know.

"Now, will you be good and tell Miss Wells what I have said?" he asked.

"Yes, Father," I said again. But inside I was not saying *yes* at all.

He opened the door to Daisy's eager face, and ushered her inside again.

"What a bother!" said Daisy as the door closed behind him. "Is your father very cross?"

"Very," I said. "He's banned us from having anything to do with the murder."

"He's not likely to forget at all, is he? Sometimes Daddy—"

"No," I said gloomily. "He never forgets *anything* except Mother's birthday, and I think that's on purpose."

"Well, we shall just have to be extra careful, then," said Daisy.

"*Extra* careful," I agreed. "You know my father doesn't like to be disobeyed, Daisy. And he's . . . a noticing sort of person."

"Well," said Daisy, "So's Mrs. Vitellius, and yet we managed to discover the spy under her very nose today. This will only be more of the same. We must just imagine ourselves in enemy territory, under surveillance by particularly cunning foes. We can't give up."

"I know," I said. I really did. Detective work is frightening, but what happened at Fallingford has made me realize that terrible things happen whether or not you want them to. You must make a choice: to turn and look them in the eye, and see the terrible things for what they are, or to hide away and pretend to yourself that they are not real—and if you choose the second, there is always a moment when you can't pretend any more. Last term, I decided that I was not going to be the kind of person who pretended. I would square my shoulders, and be, if not heroic (I have explained before that I am not someone who can ever be heroic, really), then at least very brave.

"We're going to find the murderer," said Daisy. "We'll just have to be very clever about how we do it, that's all."

There was a brisk, Hetty-shaped knock on the door, and then Hetty herself popped her head round it. Her cap was on slightly askew, and her cheeks were pink with emotion. She looked afraid, and hectic, and secretly excited—just the way I felt.

"Mr. Wong came looking for me," she said, "to tell me to watch over you. Oh, Miss Daisy, can't you ever stop poking your nose in?"

I wondered again why people always assumed that it was Daisy, not me, who caused all the trouble.

"I'm to make sure that you get into bed and don't listen to all the nasty stuff in the corridor. Miss Hazel, your father's fuming."

"This is all most unfair!" said Daisy, the picture of injured innocence.

"Oh, it is not," said Hetty, grinning and tucking a stray

strand of red hair up into her cap. "I know you, Miss Daisy. You brought this upon yourself."

"Hetty, you won't really stop us from looking into things, will you?" asked Daisy. "It's so dull, following the rules all the time."

Hetty looked uncomfortable. "If you want to get up to mischief, I won't enquire, but I can't help you do it. While I'm on this holiday I work for Miss Hazel's father. I'm sorry, Miss Daisy, but that's the way it is."

It was not fair! I thought as Hetty called in an attendant to fold down our bunks, and then tidied away our things while we changed into our nighties.

I climbed up to the top bunk (Daisy says she needs the bottom bunk, in case anything happens that she wants to investigate) and Hetty tucked the sheets in around me. Her thin hands were rough, and reminded me of our family's *mui jai*, back in Hong Kong. I smiled at her.

"Hetty," said Daisy below me, and I heard her sit up. "Sarah must be upset about what happened to Mrs. Daunt."

"Is that a question?" asked Hetty.

"Of course not!" said Daisy. "But she is, isn't she?"

"Hmm," said Hetty, climbing back down the ladder with one final smile at me. She vanished from sight, and I had to wriggle round a bit to bring the room back into view below me. "Some people don't show their emotions on the outside, you know that."

"So she's not upset?"

"She's busy, Miss Daisy! Mr. Daunt needs looking after, and Mrs. Daunt . . . Well, I heard she wasn't the best of mistresses. Never gave Sarah anything by way of perks. Not that I think Sarah should take things from her—"

"What things?"

"Oh, only little trinkets—I shouldn't have told you that. No using it in your investigation!"

"Hetty, will you watch her?"

"Miss Daisy!" said Hetty. "Don't! Miss Livedon won't like it. I've seen her looking at you."

So Hetty *had* noticed who Mrs. Vitellius really was. "Hetty!" said Daisy, propping herself up on her elbows. "This is really most important—we'll keep mum about Sarah and the stealing, but *you* mustn't say anything to anyone about where you've met Miss Livedon—Mrs. Vitellius—before! She's on a really top-secret mission."

"I never would," said Hetty. "Although not for her sake."

Hetty, as I have said, really is an utter brick.

"Now, lights out, girls. I'll be back in the morning—and I shall be listening hard tonight. No talking!"

"Yes, Hetty," said Daisy. "Of course."

But as soon as she had gone I felt a knocking on the wooden slats underneath my bunk. It only took me a moment to recognize the Morse code pattern:

I-n-v-e-s-t-i-g-a-t-i-o-n-b-e-g-i-n-s-t-o-m-o-r-r-o-w!

Y-e-s, I knocked back, light as a whisper.

D-e-t-e-c-t-i-v-e-s-o-c-i-e-t-y-f-o-r-e-v-e-r, knocked Daisy, and then I heard her sigh happily, and roll over, and fall asleep. Life, for Daisy, is never better than when we are on a case.

I, however, could not sleep. I wrote everything up, until my wristwatch, hanging on its hook next to my bunk, said 12:20, and the stopped train, slowly at first and then faster and faster, began to huff and churn and gallop forward again through the night. Daisy rolled over in bed and muttered, "Unhand me, criminal, I know the truth!"

I jumped, then giggled. Of course, she was only having a dream. I lay still a while longer, feeling the train jolting about beneath me, and then my eyes began to drift closed. I shut them properly, and saw the floating blackness behind my eyelids and then nothing at all.

Robin Stevens

Part Three
We Are Stopped in Our Tracks

I woke with a jump. I thought I'd been dreaming something horrid about the night before—but then I realized that the jumping was carrying on even though I was awake; an awful loud howling and juddering, as though the Orient Express itself were being tortured.

"Lord!" said Daisy from below me. "Why are we stopping?"

"I don't know!" I said, my teeth chattering. "It isn't morning yet!"

It wasn't. My wristwatch said 5:14, and the light filtering through our blind was still pearlish.

I climbed down from my bunk, the rungs pressing coldly up against my bare feet, and then splashed water from the basin onto my face and neck (I missed the bit behind my ears, but decided that it was allowed, under the circumstances). Daisy was hopping from foot to foot, desperate to get out of the door. Her hair was brushed and her robe was neatly tied. I reminded myself for the hundredth time that

Daisy Wells does not really have magical beautifying powers.

"All right!" I said, pulling on my own pale blue robe. "All right, I'm coming!" and we pushed the door open and peered out into the corridor.

Other doors were opening now too, and guests were appearing, all wrapped in robes and slippers. The Countess, leaning on her cane, was majestic in an eau-de-nil silk creation, and Mrs. Vitellius was draped in a beautiful duck-egg blue kimono. Alexander, in surprisingly childish pinstriped pajamas which he was slightly too tall for, began to smile at us, but then the Countess said, "Alexander! Do not look at the ladies, if you please!" and he blushed until his ears went red. Daisy dropped a curtsey in the Countess's direction, and I saw them eyeing each other approvingly.

"Whatever's the matter?" growled Mr. Daunt, in a velvety purple robe like an emperor. "Where is that man Jocelyn! Why have we stopped?"

At the sound of his voice, Jocelyn came hurrying up, fully dressed even though it was so dreadfully early. His face was creased with concern.

"Ladies," he said, "gentlemen—my apologies. There has been a sudden stop—it is quite necessary—you are all safe, let me assure you—"

"Safe?" said the Countess as Madame Melinda appeared in a black dressing gown as fringed and fanciful as her day dress had been. "Why should we not be safe?"

"Ladies—gentlemen—let me assure you . . ." There was something Jocelyn did not want to say to us, I could tell.

"SPIT IT OUT, MAN!" roared Mr. Daunt.

Jocelyn took a deep breath. "Ladies and gentlemen," he said. "Do not be alarmed."

I heard another door opening, and Mr. Strange poked his head out. His face looked drawn and pale, and his thin fingers gripped the edge of his door. Why did he seem so afraid all the time? I wondered. What was going on inside his head? Seeing Mr. Strange made me realize who was missing—once again, Il Mysterioso's door remained firmly closed. Where was he? It was impossible that he had failed to hear all the commotion in the corridor.

"We are still in Jugo-Slavia, I'm afraid. Near Vincovci, just this side of the border. I cannot tell you when we'll be moving again. There's been . . . Ladies and gentlemen, a device has exploded on the line up ahead."

I was quite sure that I had misheard him. After all, it seemed too dramatic to be true—just like something out of one of Daisy's spy novels. But then the Countess sucked in her breath, and Mrs. Vitellius shrieked, and I knew that they had heard the same words I had. A device. A *bomb*.

"This is too much!" cried Sarah. She went pushing through the crowd to Mr. Daunt's side. "First murder, now explosions—I shall hand in my notice!"

"Quiet, Sarah," snapped Mr. Daunt, catching hold of her arm. I noticed them staring at each other; he did not let her go straight away.

"It's the Soviets!" shrieked the Countess, clutching her throat. "Alexander! Quick!"

"Madam!" cried Jocelyn, waving his arms so that the buttons on his wagon-lit uniform flashed. "It is not the Soviets! It is merely rebels, trying to make trouble in their country! You are in no danger. Please listen to me!"

"DESIST!" my father roared suddenly, and everyone else fell silent and froze, shocked.

"Thank you, sir," said Jocelyn. "Ladies and gentlemen, please. Do not fear. You are perfectly safe. This is something we were warned of—this was the matter I was discussing in the other carriage last night when the, ah, very unfortunate incident occurred—but we had hoped to avoid an explosion. Luckily, however, although the bomb was meant to destroy the line, the actions of our scouting party caused it to have only minimal damage. We are now fixing this, and we shall be on our way in the next day or so."

"The next *day* or so!" cried Madame Melinda. "But—" The grown-ups all began to panic. Sarah was threatening to hand in her notice again, and Mr. Daunt was shouting at her in a way that really was very rude. I wondered if I had imagined the arm-holding moment. "If there really *was* a bomb on the line," whispered Daisy to me, "then

116   *Robin Stevens*

we're stuck here until it's fixed, and *that* means we can't get to the police. We're all alone again, which makes it far easier to detect, even if we do have Mrs. Vitellius and your father trying to stop us. Hazel, this case may not have got off to the best start, but things are looking up at last!"

Unfortunately, she had spoken too soon.

Still in our night things, we were all asked to gather at our tables in the dining car, sitting just as we had the evening before (the gap where Mrs. Daunt had been loomed so large that no one could look at it). Jocelyn stood at one end, and next to him stood the doctor from the Calais–Athens coach. He looked just as confident as he had last night—not, as I knew Kitty would have said to me if she had been there (I had a sudden moment of missing her), that he had much reason for it. He was a thin man, with rather a large head and ears that stuck out, and his suit did not fit.

Il Mysterioso had at last been ferreted out of his compartment. He did not explain why he hadn't emerged earlier; in fact, he did not speak at all. He sat with his shoulders hunched beneath his cloak, playing a coin to and fro between his fingers. He looked pale and pointed, and his beard was quite uncombed. I supposed that he was upset that we'd been prevented from reaching Belgrade, so he couldn't hand over his documents. I reminded myself that he could not know that Daisy and I knew his secret, but all the same I shivered when he happened to raise his eyes and stare at me.

"Ladies and gentlemen," said Jocelyn, smoothing down his jacket. "As you know, the train is not moving at present. This is for your safety.

"In light of the events of last night, we are in a rather delicate situation. The, er, body has been moved into the guards' van, and will be safe there until we arrive in Belgrade, but the fact remains that a crime has been committed, and of course it must be looked into. Luckily I have discovered that we happen to have a—well—someone with experience of these matters on board."

Mrs. Vitellius coughed daintily into her handkerchief and I glanced at her in shock. Had she revealed her identity to Jocelyn?

Daisy sat up very straight and pinched my arm, pink-cheeked. I realized what she was thinking. She was quite obviously ready for the Detective Society to be officially given the case. "We're it, Hazel!" she murmured. "Buck up!"

"I am bucked," I said. "It's only that I haven't eaten breakfast yet. And are you sure—"

"Of course I'm sure!" hissed Daisy—and then her mouth dropped open as Jocelyn turned, not to Mrs. Vitellius's table, or ours—but to the doctor beside him.

"This," he said, "is Dr. Sandwich, graduate of medicine and, it emerges, an amateur detective of some repute. He solved last year's Satterthwaite murder—you must recall?"

Everyone looked blank.

"I had only a small hand in the matter," said Dr. Sandwich, wriggling his thin shoulders under his suit. I noticed that his nose bulged, and he had a little moustache and stubby eyelashes that fluttered when he spoke. "I . . . was able to advise the police."

"You told me you solved the case!" exclaimed Jocelyn.

"Well," said Dr. Sandwich. "Perhaps. I did deduce that the size and position of the wound meant that the supposed murder weapon, a fire iron, could not have been used. Instead, Mr. Satterthwaite must have been killed with an antique paperweight from the family collection—and that pointed to only one murderer."

He paused. "It was really quite easy," he said, with false modesty.

Daisy's grip on my arm had suddenly become painful. "Ow!" I mouthed at her. I do not think she heard.

"Ladies and gentlemen," said Jocelyn, "I have been allowed by my superiors to nominate Dr. Sandwich as the representative of the international police until the train reaches Belgrade. He has already examined the crime scene, allowing the body to be moved to its present position, and he now requests that you allow yourselves to be interviewed in this dining car. After breakfast you will be called in one by one—until you are, we ask you to remain calmly in your compartments. There is no reason to be concerned—on behalf of the Compagnie Internationale des Wagons-Lits, I can promise you that you will suffer no more disruption than necessary. We aim to make your stay with us as secure and comfortable as possible. The one request I must make is that you do not lock your doors—it is important that everything remains open and accessible to Dr. Sandwich."

"And what if we refuse?" asked Mr. Strange quietly. He was very pale and his hands were shaking. He did not look either secure or comfortable.

"You wouldn't dare!" said Mr. Daunt loudly. "You haven't given any alibi for the moment Georgie was killed, have you? Do you know"—he turned to Dr. Sandwich—"that he wrote to Georgie and asked her for two hundred pounds just a week ago? Of course she refused, as I told her she must, and he must have followed us onto the train so he could ask her again!"

"I had no idea you would be here!" cried Mr. Strange. "This was a . . . a research trip. I—"

"Please," said Jocelyn. "Please—wait for the interviews."

"Very well," said Mr. Daunt. "But I demand to go first."

Jocelyn nodded, palms together. "Now, if you are amenable, I shall call for the breakfast service. Thank you all—and please, as I said, do not fear!"

Of course, most people ignored his assurances. Madame Melinda was talking about negative energy and dangerous forces. Sarah was muttering furiously, her arms crossed, and Mr. Daunt was glaring at Madame Melinda. Alexander was fiddling with his pajama cuff. Then he looked up at Jocelyn and Dr. Sandwich, and I caught his expression. It was shiningly excited, the same look that Daisy gets when we talk about detection.

"Excuse me," said Alexander to Dr. Sandwich. "Excuse me! I'd like to help."

Robin Stevens

lexander!" snapped the Countess. "Do not be ridiculous!"

But Dr. Sandwich held up a hand. "Wait," he said, his eyes—like his nose, they were rather large and bulging—fixing on Alexander. "Young man, why do you want to aid us?"

"I want to be a detective when I grow up," said Alexander. "I already have lots of useful skills. I can even almost write shorthand. I've been learning it out of a book."

"That is commendable, but I'm afraid we cannot let you help," said Jocelyn.

"No, no, Mr. Buri," said Dr. Sandwich. "Wait. The lad wants to help—why shouldn't he? He ought to be rewarded for his noble offer—and I can already tell that he has great potential. Why, he reminds me of myself at his age. Yes, Mr. Arcady, you may be our personal stenographer."

The Countess opened and closed her mouth; for once

she had no sharp, cutting remark ready. Her fingers in their little bed-gloves clasped the table. I stared at her. Was she upset because she didn't want her grandson mixed up with a murder mystery? Or was she afraid of what he might discover about *her*? "Alexander," she said at last, in a surprisingly small voice, "I don't—"

"My lady!" cried Dr. Sandwich. "You must let him! Why, anyone would think you had something to hide!"

He chuckled jovially.

The Countess swallowed. She had given in.

"Excuse me! May I point out that my secretary has a shorthand qualification and a traveling typewriter," said my father, frowning. "Would he not be more useful?"

"Nonsense! We already have our helper," said Dr. Sandwich. "We are not the police—we can afford to employ more unconventional methods."

I decided that I disliked him.

I looked at Daisy to see what she made of him. She was staring off into the distance, her chin in her hand like a pretty portrait. Only I could hear her grinding her teeth. I nudged her and the grinding stopped.

We were sent back to our compartments to get dressed and wait for breakfast—and of course, Daisy was fuming. "This is simply the worst holiday I've ever been on!" she hissed. "Alexander gets to hear all about the murder while we're not allowed to investigate at *all*."

Robin Stevens

"Shh," I said. "Someone will hear you."

"No chance of that! We're surrounded by fools," said Daisy. She really was in a mood.

For once, breakfast lasted far longer than I would have liked. A constant stream of waiters flowed through the dining car with pots of coffee and salvers piled high with good things, but without the noise of the train clacking along the rails everything was eerily silent. No one spoke, and no one dared to look up, in case they caught someone else's eye.

And I knew why. One of the people in the Calais–Istanbul coach must be the murderer—that was quite obvious, even to the grown-ups.

Ours was the very front carriage of the train. There was no carriage beyond ours, so there was no reason for any other passenger to walk through it—it didn't lead anywhere. And anyway, no other passenger had left the dining car during dinner and gone into our sleeping car—they would have had to walk past our tables, and we would have noticed.

So who had been absent from the dining car at the moment Mrs. Daunt screamed?

I took a pastry from one of the platters and decided that, while we waited for the right moment to hold our first detective meeting, I could organize things in my head so that I was ready for it. I took a large bite of pastry (with extra apricot jam heaped on top) and stared at the nibblers and sippers and pickers around me. Once again, I could not understand why murder seemed to ruin some people's appetites. Then I made myself think back to the evening before.

There had been the four of us at our table: me, Daisy, Father, and Maxwell. Next to us, at the Daunts' table, had been Mr. Daunt, alone once Mrs. Daunt had left. On the same side, closer to the kitchen, Sarah had gone out, leaving Hetty alone, and next to them, the Countess had left Alexander alone at their table. Between our table and the door, Mr. Strange, Il Mysterioso, Mrs. Vitellius, and Madame Melinda had all gone—their table of four had been quite empty.

As I was thinking this, letting the night before fill up my head until I could almost see it when I squinted, I happened to glance down at Daisy's plate. She had left her final piece of toast, and now she was breaking it up into crumbs and pushing them about in vague patterns. I had never seen Daisy pick at her food—it was most out of character. But then I looked at those crumbs again, and saw that the patterns she was making were not random. The pieces of toast were grouped in three sets of two and two sets of four, arranged just like our real tables. As I watched, Daisy took away one complete four and one from each of the twos. She looked up at me, face very straight, for all the world as though she were bored, and could not think how better to occupy her time—and then she spread her hands out on the tablecloth with both thumbs and two fingers tucked under.

Daisy was telling me, as clear as day, that we had six possible suspects—and who those suspects were. Il Mysterioso, Mr. Strange, Madame Melinda, Mrs. Vitellius, Sarah, and the Countess. Judging by the evidence of our own eyes and ears, no one else could have done it.

After breakfast I assumed that we would be left alone to hold our detective meeting—but my father had other plans. "Hazel," he said. "Miss Wells. Why don't we all sit together this morning? Bring your things through to Maxwell's compartment."

I knew that he was trying to protect us while the investigation was going on, but I burned with shame. He was treating us like little children! How scornful Daisy would be. Why, her parents didn't—But then I caught myself.

"How wizard!" said Daisy, with her best enthusiastic face on. "We can fill out our puzzle books, can't we, Hazel!"

I looked at her and caught her tiny wink. "Oh," I said. "Yes. Our puzzle books."

"Splendid!" said my father, squeezing my shoulder. I smiled up at him awkwardly. But of course there was nothing to do but bring our things to Maxwell's compartment,

Hetty following along behind with an armful of puzzle books and novels (she was careful to include none of the crime ones).

I opened *The Baffle Book* (Daisy and I have solved its puzzles so many times that it feels like an old friend) to get at this casebook, which lay inside it—and then slammed it shut again as my father came through the connecting door.

He stared down at Daisy and me, sitting on the plush seat, and I was sure that he must be able to see straight through the pages of *The Baffle Book* and realize that we were disobeying him. But he only pushed his glasses up his nose and said, "Good, you are settling in. Now, there are papers I must work on this morning—will you be all right here? Maxwell and I will be just on the other side of this door."

"Yes, Father," I replied.

"Yes, Mr. Wong," said Daisy, with a dazzling smile.

My father went back into his compartment, leaving the door ajar. A moment later we heard him say to Maxwell, "Now, the Darlington letter. Further to his correspondence on the twenty-seventh of last month . . ."

"I think you'll agree that we have a new nemesis," said Daisy, quiet as a breath. "Dr. Sandwich. What an . . . an amateur! We must prove ourselves better than him!"

"Shh!" I mouthed, and in the other room my father raised his voice to ask, "Are you all right, girls?"

I opened *The Baffle Book* on my knee with my casebook inside, and, nudging Daisy, wrote:

I agree. But we can't talk. Why don't I begin our suspect list–and you can stop me if I write anything wrong. All right?

Daisy frowned. Then she seized the pencil from me and wrote:

All right. But I'm writing some of the entries.

I nodded, and the quietest ever meeting of the Detective Society began.

Present: Daisy Wells, president, and Hazel Wong, vice president and secretary.
To be investigated: The case of Mrs. Daunt's murder.
Date of death: Sunday 7 July 1935.
Time of death:

I paused. Daisy immediately snatched the pencil from me and wrote:

8:31 p.m.

I shrugged at her, amazed. She pointed to her wristwatch and rolled her eyes. Of course—as soon as she heard the scream, she must have checked her watch. It was an utterly Daisy-ish thing to do.

Time of death: 8:31 p.m.
Murder weapon: Mr. Strange's knife.
Murder method: Throat slit.

Again, I knew that only too well. I thought of the blood, all over Mrs. Daunt and the floor and her lovely dinner dress. What I had seen in that compartment was so horrid that, after the initial shock, it hardly seemed real. The doorway had been a sort of frame that separated me from what was happening inside. Mrs. Daunt had looked, not like a human, but a doll, the blood comically red, as though it had been spread about by someone playing a joke. And all the shouting around me had seemed like lines being spoken in a radio play, very loud and dramatic but not really meaning anything.

I found a body once, almost a year ago. There was not much blood at all, and no screaming; only someone lying very still in the half-dark—but it is in my mind as the worst horror there could be. It still makes my skin crawl.

Mr. Strange. MOTIVE: He is Mrs. Daunt's brother, and did not get any money from their mother's will. She got everything. He does not seem to be making any money from his books either. Therefore he might have killed Mrs. Daunt because he hoped to get something from her will; or he might have killed her out of spite or jealousy for having been overlooked. NOTES: His knife was the murder weapon. He said it was stolen—is this true? He was in the sleeping car at the moment when Mrs. Daunt screamed. He writes crime novels—is this suspicious? He says he did not know that the Daunts would be on the train—is this true?

Daisy snatched the pencil again and wrote:

Doubtful.

I could see that she agreed: Mr. Strange was a very likely suspect.

The Countess. MOTIVE: She believes that Mrs. Daunt's ruby necklace is really hers. The necklace is now missing. Did she kill Mrs. Daunt to steal it? NOTES: She was

Robin Stevens

in the sleeping car at the moment when Mrs. Daunt screamed.

Il Mysterioso. MOTIVE: We believe that he is the spy Mrs. Vitellius is investigating. Did Mrs. Daunt discover his secret, forcing him to silence her? NOTES: He was in the sleeping car at the moment when Mrs. Daunt screamed, but he did not appear in the corridor when Mrs. Daunt's body was discovered, despite the noise. Why did he stay in his compartment?

Daisy scrawled:

And he is a magician—who else would be able to perform a locked-room trick so well?

I nodded at her. I remembered Il Mysterioso's trick for the policemen the afternoon before. In light of what had happened to Mrs. Daunt, it did not seem so innocent any more.

Madame Melinda. MOTIVE: We know that Mrs. Daunt was paying her to contact her dead mother, and Mr. Daunt did not like it. He was trying to get his wife away from Madame Melinda-Madame Melinda can't have wanted to lose Mrs. Daunt's money. Might she have thought that she would gain from Mrs. Daunt's will?

NOTES: She was in the sleeping car at the moment when Mrs. Daunt screamed. She also used to be an actress—Il Mysterioso said so—so she must be very good at pretending.

Daisy pinched me appreciatively at that.

Sarah. MOTIVE: She seemed to dislike Mrs. Daunt. We know from Hetty that she was stealing from her, and we saw her threatening to give in her notice. But is unhappiness with her job enough to make her kill her mistress? Or did Mrs. Daunt find out about the thefts and threaten to hand her over to the police? NOTES: She was in the sleeping car at the moment when Mrs. Daunt screamed.

Those were the five suspects that I was certain of. Now we came to the one who concerned me.

Mrs. Vitellius. MOTIVE: None that we can see yet. But we know that she is not who others believe her to be. She was also in the sleeping car at the moment when Mrs Daunt screamed.

I looked at Daisy to see if she really thought that Mrs Vitellius might be responsible.

Robin Stevens

She raised her eyebrows and shrugged. Then she wrote,

You never know. What if Mrs. Daunt were the spy?

I had not thought of that. Surely not even Mrs. Vitellius would be allowed to kill someone in the course of her job. . . . But although I did not believe it, we could not discount her until we had proved to ourselves that she had not done it. That was part of our Detective Society code.

So there were our six suspects, and there were their motives. But how were we to rule five of them out? I shrugged at Daisy, as if to say, *What next?*

She rolled her eyes at me again—I rather resented that—and took up the pencil.

PLAN OF ACTION

1. Speak to Mrs. Vitellius and ask her for her full alibi. She ought also to be able to show us her letter of reference from the government.
2. Find Mrs. Daunt's will to see who gains from her death.
3. Gain access to the dining-car interviews.
4. Obtain clues.
5. Recreate the crime.

I raised both eyebrows at that list. I did not see how we were to accomplish 2 and 3—and even 4 and 5 seemed very hopeful.

Despite Daisy's optimism, I felt that we really were stuck. And then someone knocked on my father's door.

Robin Stevens

We heard it through the half-open connecting door, and the wall (they really were very thin, the partitions between compartments).

"Come in!" called my father.

"Oh, Mr. Wong!" said Mrs. Vitellius in her sweetest voice. My heart jumped, and Daisy and I stared at each other. What did it mean? "Good morning. I'm so sorry, did I disturb you?"

"Not at all," said my father. "How may I help you?"

"Well . . . you see, I have just had some elevenses delivered to my compartment, and it really is rather enormous. Much too much for me! And I thought, why, perhaps I could invite your two girls in to help me eat it? What with the *awful things* that have happened, I thought it might be nice to give them a little distraction."

"How kind of you!" said my father. "But—"

"Oh, we'll be perfectly safe," said Mrs. Vitellius. "It will take their mind off things, I'm sure. We can talk about dresses—it will be *such* fun!"

"Hmm," said my father. He does not approve of me thinking about clothes too much—he says that it distracts me from important things like history and sums. I'm sure I can think of both. But I heard the note in his voice that meant he was about to agree. "Very well, then. They are through that door, in my secretary's compartment—and no doubt listening in. But keep a close eye on them, won't you? It's been . . . Well, you know what has been happening."

I heard the sound of Mrs. Vitellius's high-heeled footsteps, and then she popped her head round the connecting door, in her tangerine dress, even more striking than yesterday's.

"Girls!" she said. "How should you like to come with me and eat cake?"

Daisy and I were ushered along the corridor. I felt horribly prisoner-like, even when we went into Mrs. Vitellius's compartment and saw what was waiting for us there: in the middle of the room, on a handsome wooden stand, was a great silver tray, piled high with creamy cakes and little fruit tarts and iced fancies. Three china cups stood ready next to an enormous silver jug, which steamed deliciously. Mrs. Vitellius had obviously been expecting us.

Robin Stevens

We sat down, and she poured, flooding the whole room with the spicy smell of chocolate. It was hardly hot chocolate weather—the compartment was already warm, with the sun pouring in through the window—but I did not mind. It looked glorious.

Mrs. Vitellius leaned forward and took the plumpest, creamiest cake, absolutely oozing with jam. "Go on, girls," she said, winking at us. "I know how you like your bun-breaks."

"Is this a trick?" asked Daisy, folding her arms.

I folded my arms too, in solidarity with her, and tried not to gaze at the cakes. I knew what Daisy would say: that a good detective must never put personal comfort before the needs of an investigation. But they did look excellent.

"This," said Mrs. Vitellius, "is a discussion. Is that all right with you?"

"No," said Daisy, sticking her chin out. "I don't like it. Before we go any further I want you to show us your official letter from *him*—the person we shall call M. Just so we know that you really *are* doing what you say you are, and it's all right. *And* you can give us your alibi as well."

Mrs. Vitellius glared at us, all jolly pretense dropped. "You girls!" she began. Then she sighed, reached into her fashionable little clutch bag and pulled out a piece of paper. "Here you are," she said. "From M himself, officially confirming that I am here to do the business of the British government—and not murder anyone, in case that was what you were thinking."

I craned over Daisy's shoulder, and we read the letter together. It was typed on thick cream paper with a beautiful lion and unicorn crest.

TO WHOM IT MAY CONCERN

The woman who has given you this letter is LUCY LIVEDON, member of the Metropolitan Police Force, and she has OFFICIAL DISPENSATION to travel without let or hindrance throughout Europe in pursuit of the spy code-named OYSTER, wanted by the British government on suspicion of passing classified information between European nations. Miss Livedon is not to be harmed or prevented from carrying out her mission—you are ordered to comply with her requests and allow her safe passage, in the name of KING GEORGE V, Supreme Ruler of the British Empire. M.

"Well," said Daisy. "That all seems to be in order. And your alibi? If we're not satisfied, I warn you, we can scream terribly loudly."

"Daisy, don't be ridiculous."

"I'm not! *I'm* not the person on a top-secret mission which could be compromised at any moment."

"Very well," snapped Mrs. Vitellius. "As you no doubt already noticed, I left the dining car last night with Madame Melinda, who is in the next compartment to mine. Tiresome woman. She saw me to my door, and when I went in I heard her muttering away to herself. It was so loud that I knocked to quiet her—and a moment later I heard the scream. I ran out of my compartment at the same moment that Madame Melinda came out of hers. Happy?"

Daisy frowned. "It sounds plausible," she said. "We shall have to compare your story with Madame Melinda's before we accept it absolutely, of course, but it will do for now."

I agreed with her. We would have to hear from Madame Melinda in order to be utterly sure, but if she confirmed the story, it seemed as though we could rule out not only Mrs. Vitellius, but Madame Melinda as well. "Did you hear anyone running past your compartment after the scream, by the way?" asked Daisy.

"I did not," said Mrs. Vitellius. "Which does not mean it didn't happen, of course—the murderer could have removed their shoes—they wouldn't have been heard on the carpet. I expect the murderer dodged into their own compartment, and then rejoined the crowd in the corridor once it was large enough. Now that I have cleared up the matter of my innocence, may I speak about why I called you here?"

"All right then," said Daisy. "If you must."

I picked up my fondant fancy at last and bit into it,

letting the sugar melt against my tongue. Uncomfortable situations, I feel, are always made slightly less so by food.

"I want to speak to you about the murder. It's a dangerous business, girls."

"We know that!" said Daisy scornfully.

"Well then, it should be only too obvious that if you want to keep yourselves safe you must have nothing further to do with it," said Mrs. Vitellius. "I know you're cross with me for getting your father to prevent you detecting—but this is no place for you. Whether or not the murder is linked to the case I was ordered on to this train to investigate—"

"Oh, do you think it is?" asked Daisy brightly.

Mrs. Vitellius glared at her before continuing, "As a representative of the British government, I must now investigate this murder of a British citizen, and I don't want you dragged into it. I know you girls solved the Fallingford murder, but this is quite different."

"How is it different?" asked Daisy heatedly. The wrinkle had appeared on the bridge of her nose, just as I knew it would. "Anyway, we're part of it now. We were there when it happened! And we haven't just solved the Fallingford murder. We have solved *two* murder cases. We are *detectives*. We have badges!"

"I know, Daisy," said Mrs. Vitellius, sighing again. "But I have to think about what M would want, and I know that although he trusts you—"

"If he trusts us, then *you* should!" cried Daisy, putting down her fondant fancy. "This simply isn't fair of you! You're being awful! You shouldn't be stopping us detecting, you should be helping us. We can't leave everything to that dreadful Dr. Sandwich. We're much better detectives than he is, and you know it."

Mrs. Vitellius sucked in a breath. Her nostrils pinched in and she drew her eyebrows together. "Daisy Wells!" she said. "You are a very difficult child."

"I'm not a child, I'm a detective, and if you ban us from detecting I shall tell the whole carriage who you really are. I don't want to, but I will if you make me," said Daisy, folding her arms again. "Heroes often have to do rather awful things to make sure that everything turns out all right in the end."

"Stay out of this case!" snapped Mrs. Vitellius. "If I catch you poking your noses in, I shall do my very best to stop you."

They glared at each other, and I realized that if I did not say something we might be stuck here forever. Neither of them was the sort to give in.

"What if we promised to stay safe?" I asked. "We don't want to be hurt any more than you do." (This was not entirely true. Daisy does not mind the idea of being hurt simply because she does not believe in danger. She imagines herself the heroine of her story, and everyone knows that heroines cannot die.) "If we stay safe, and you don't see us detecting—isn't that enough?"

Mrs. Vitellius opened her mouth to say *no*. But then she took a deep breath. "You'll stay away from the spy?" she asked.

"Unless they turn out to be the murderer, yes," said Daisy grandly.

Mrs. Vitellius pressed down on a piece of cake with her fork—so hard that it became a sort of paste on her plate.

"Oh!" she said. "You can be sure M will hear about this! You are dreadful."

"Only when someone crosses us," said Daisy cheerfully. "Don't worry, you shan't hear a peep out of us until we solve the case."

"Until *I* solve the case, you mean," said Mrs Vitellius. They glared at each other again.

"Well," Mrs. Vitellius went on, "the one thing we *can* agree on is that it won't be Dr. Sandwich. The man's a fool of the first degree. If it were up to him, the murder would never be solved."

VI

Now that we seemed to have almost reached an agreement, I took a fruit tart and nibbled at it thoughtfully. I wondered again whether Mrs. Vitellius knew as much as we did about the spy. Ought we to tell her what we had seen in Milan, and what we suspected about Il Mysterioso? But no, Daisy would be furious with me.

The room was very warm now, what with the hot chocolate and the three of us crammed into it. I looked at the window and wished it would open properly. Everything on this train was so close—it was really horrid to think how near the murderer must be, only separated from us by a few doors, and none of them locked.

That made me think of the locked-room mystery, of course. If Daisy was right, the murderer we were up against this time had planned what they had done, quite carefully—could we really be safe if we tried to unmask the culprit? How long would it take for them to realize that we were on their track?

I jumped when there was a knock on the door. "Come in!" called Mrs. Vitellius, and the door opened to reveal Hetty. She was shifting from foot to foot, looking most concerned. I suddenly realized how odd this must be for her. Luckily, she is very good in odd situations.

"Good morning, Mrs. Vitellius," she said. "I've been sent by Miss Wong's father to collect the girls from you."

"We were having a lovely time, weren't we, girls?" said Mrs. Vitellius. "Thank you, Letty—oh, no, Hetty."

"Yes, madam," said Hetty, deadpan. "If I may, madam . . . Come along, girls. You're to come back to Mr. Wong's compartment."

It was an order—yet another one—from a grown-up who meant well but who was hampering our efforts to investigate the case. I glanced back at Mrs. Vitellius as we left, and I thought she looked rather cheerful. She knew that she had the head start on us—how could we hope to solve the case before she did?

Robin Stevens

VII

We sat down in our old places in Maxwell's compartment. I was still struggling to understand how the murder had happened at all. How could the murderer have locked both Mrs. Daunt's main door and the connecting door, then somehow manage to get out of the room and escape without anyone seeing or hearing them? Even though Jocelyn had been in the Calais–Athens coach when the murder had happened, surely one of the other passengers would have seen the murderer? Only a few moments had passed between Mrs. Daunt's scream and everyone in the dining car rushing along to her compartment. It seemed like a magic trick, or something from a murder mystery novel—but was the fact that we had a magician and a crime writer amongst our suspects important, or just a red herring?

Daisy seized the casebook and wrote, crossly:

So many questions!

I nodded and wrote:

How did the murderer escape from a locked room? Mr. Daunt had to break down the main door to get into the compartment, so we know that was locked from the inside. That door could only be locked from the inside by someone in the room sliding the bolt across, or from the outside using a wagon-lit attendant's master key, and we had heard Jocelyn say that none of the master keys had gone missing. And we saw Madame Melinda unlock the connecting door when she wanted to get into Mr. Daunt's compartment and lie down for a moment-so we know that someone must have locked it from Mrs. Daunt's side. The windows don't open properly, we both know that too, and we saw that the room was empty apart from Mrs. Daunt. There isn't anywhere to hide in those compartments-so how did the murderer manage to kill Mrs. Daunt and escape without anyone noticing?

"Yes!" said Daisy. We both automatically looked up at the connecting door to my father's compartment. Just like

Robin Stevens

the one between Mr. and Mrs. Daunt's compartments, each side had a shiny silver bolt—it could be locked by either person, or both at once. There was no way for anyone on one side of the door to push back the bolt if it was locked on the other side. Madame Melinda had been able to open the door the evening before because only Mrs. Daunt had pushed her bolt home—on Mr. Daunt's side it was unlocked.

So could someone have set it up to allow them to close the bolt from the other side? If they had tied a bit of string to the bolt, perhaps, closed the door and tugged on the string to pull the bolt home?

I stood up, the better to peer at the connecting door's bolt, and Daisy came to stand next to me. I pointed at the bolt, and mimed tying on a bit of string.

I saw that it could be done: there was a handle on the bolt to attach it to. Quick as a flash, Daisy was kneeling down to undo her shoelace. She wrapped it round the bolt in a clever little knot, and then handed the other end to me with a nod. I realized what she wanted me to do. I stepped through the doorway, lace tucked into my hand, and pulled the door closed behind me. Maxwell and my father looked up, surprised.

"Hello," I said, rather weakly, and gave the string in my hand a sharp tug. The bolt caught, and I tugged again—and there was a click. I had done it.

"Are you all right, Hazel?" asked my father.

"Er," I said. "Yes. I just wanted to come and see you." Daisy's knot was not coming undone. I pulled at it once more, and stepped into the room, to put even more pressure on it. At last I felt it give, and it slipped through the door to hang from my fingers. I balled it up in my fist and said, "Mrs. Vitellius was very nice. She gave us cake."

"Good, Hazel," said my father, eyebrows raised. "Do you need anything?"

"Er," I said again. "No. I just wanted . . . to say hello."

"Hello." He smiled at me. "Bearing up, are you?"

I nodded. "I'll—er—go back to Daisy now," I said, and only remembered then that the connecting door was locked. "Er, through the main door. It's . . . a sort of game we're playing. Goodbye."

I glanced back as I went out, and saw my father giving me a very concerned look. I could tell that he was worried that I was behaving strangely again. "Leave the door open," he called after me.

Daisy clapped me on the back as soon as I slipped into Maxwell's compartment. "Excellent!" she whispered. "You see? I have faith in you, even if you haven't. Really, you are much better than you think. We've proved that it could be done, and quite easily! That's one question answered: the locked-room trick isn't impossible after all. Now, another question: where was *the blood?*"

"Oh!" I said. I remembered all that blood—on Mrs. Daunt, on the carpet . . . So why was it that no one in the corridor—not one of our suspects—had blood on their clothes? I remembered them all, clearly lit by the chandeliers: everyone had been quite unspotted. I thought for a bit, and wrote:

No one's clothes were dirty. And there was no time for anyone to get changed.

Daisy added her comment:

They must have been covered with something while they did the awful deed. We must be on the lookout for a bloodstained bit of clothing. Perhaps a coat, or a cloak.

"Cloak!" I whispered. "Do you think—?"
"It could be," Daisy whispered back. "Put that together with the locked room—it really could be . . ."

We must get into Il Mysterioso's room and look through his possessions.

I nodded. It was funny—sitting hunched over this casebook with Daisy, snatching the pencil between us and writing over each other's words, I suddenly felt very safe and close to Deepdean—although we were miles away, in a quite alien place, surrounded by strangers.

Two more questions for you.
One: why steal the necklace, and where is it now?
Two: why, if the murderer was careful enough to lock the doors, did they forget to take the knife?

I paused to think. Then I answered:

One: either because they wanted it—or because they wanted us to think that their motive for the murder was to steal it. So, the Countess for the first reason—and any of the others for the second.

Two: I suppose the murderer might have dropped the knife as they rushed out. It could be a mistake. It could have been Mr. Strange. Or it might be quite deliberate—the murderer might really have stolen it, just the way Mr. Strange claims, and left it in the room on purpose to frame him. Everyone knew he had it with him, didn't they? We can't rule anyone out—again!

My head was spinning.

And that was when we heard voices coming from behind our heads in Il Mysterioso's compartment.

152   *Robin Stevens*

VIII

Il Mysterioso's compartment, you see, is one along from Maxwell's. They back onto one another, although they do not share a connecting door, and so, leaning our heads against the wall, we could listen in quite easily.

"Excuse me?" said Alexander's voice. "Mr. Mysterioso? Dr. Sandwich and Mr. Buri would like to see you in the dining car now."

There was a pause. "Thank you," said Il Mysterioso—and was it my imagination, or did I hear anxiety in his deep voice? "I am just coming. Wait outside."

The compartment door closed, and then there was a brief flurry of movement—a creak, a shove, as though someone were standing on the seat and shoving something onto the luggage rack—and then the door opened again and we heard Il Mysterioso's voice once more, out in the corridor this time.

"Here I am," he said. "Do your worst."

"Yes, sir," said Alexander, and then the compartment door closed, and they were gone.

Daisy and I stared at each other. We had to seize the moment somehow—but was it more important to search through Il Mysterioso's room, or eavesdrop on his interview?

"You—dining car!" hissed Daisy. "I'll go to his room!"

"No!" I whispered. "I need to stay close to my father. If he finds us gone, I can stall."

"No!" said Daisy automatically. "Oh—well—bother, Hazel, all right. But search thoroughly!"

I very nearly rolled my eyes at her, but decided at the last moment that it would be simply *too* Daisy-ish of me. Instead, as quietly as I could, I slid off the seat, its plush surface prickling my legs, and tiptoed toward the door, Daisy padding after me. In the other compartment, the voices still droned on about business.

I eased open the main door and turned left. Daisy followed me, as softly as a cat, and I tried to mimic her: no crashing, or galumphing, or unladylike movements. I do not think I did *so* badly. I slipped across the corridor carpet and pushed, very carefully, on Il Mysterioso's door, thanking everything that Jocelyn had asked for all doors to remain unlocked. It opened and, breathing in, I slid inside.

The blind was down, and the room was hushed and dark and hot. It was also chaotic: shirtfronts and collars and suit

Robin Stevens

jackets lay strewn everywhere. Since the bed had already been folded away, Il Mysterioso must have made the mess very recently. Below the mirror sat a selection of wicked little blades—I was quite horrified for a moment, until I realized that they must be beard trimmers. Next to them was a collection of square glass bottles that gave off a heavy, dangerous smell, just like Il Mysterioso himself.

I knew I had to be quick. My heart was pounding. Il Mysterioso seemed so menacing—I hated to even imagine what he might do if he found me in his room. I combed through his clothes, looking for suspicious specks of blood, but they were all quite clean. Then I looked for anything that might have provided a covering to a murderer, but although Il Mysterioso seemed to have a marvellous collection of long silk cravats and cloaks, none of them were stained. I could not see the missing necklace, either.

Then I remembered those noises we had heard, and looked at the mess again. There was something to find in this room, and I would find it. I climbed onto the folded-away bed and, on tiptoe, reached for the luggage rack. I was too short to be able to look up into it, so I had to go on the evidence of my fingers.

A large suitcase . . . a smaller one . . . a briefcase . . . and, pushed back into the far corner, a small square box that did not seem to have any hinges or openings at all. Intrigued, I lifted it down. It was a magic box—the sort that is impossible to open unless you know the trick, with a pattern of vines and fruit wriggling across the lid. It was really clever, as hiding places went—a policeman might struggle away at it for hours without making any headway at all.

However, my father has a collection back home in Hong Kong, and he used to test me on them, holding up his pocket watch and saying, "Ten minutes, Hazel . . . eleven minutes—you're slipping . . ." If there is one thing I know about, it is magic boxes. This one looked quite ordinary, as magic boxes go: I pressed its edges and tapped its side, and with a satisfying *pop!* it sprang open. Inside was a crackling packet of papers.

I squinted at them in the gloom, holding my breath and trying to hold my nerve. Were these the plans we had been looking for? Was this the final piece of proof we needed to show that Il Mysterioso was not only Mrs. Vitellius's spy, but Mrs. Daunt's murderer as well?

But it was very odd. The papers did not *look* like plans stolen from the British government. They were not even in English. I thought my eyes were playing tricks on me at first—but the letters really were all mixed-up—not Chinese, not French, not anything I could read. *Geburtstag*, I read on the first sheet, stumbling. *Charakter. Religion. Abstammung. Charakter* I could guess at, but I was not sure I was guessing correctly. *Religion* seemed straightforward—but was it one of those lying words, like *pain* in French, which means bread instead of hurt? I flipped through the pile of papers on my knee, and saw that they were all very similar: a kind of form, with different words inserted in the spaces. One word, though, came up again and again: *Katholisch*. *Katholisch. Katholisch.*

I sat still, reading and not understanding, and cross with myself for being so ignorant. I *ought* to. These were words, and words were what I was good at. Daisy would be furious at me, but I knew I could not take any of the papers with me, in case Il Mysterioso knew exactly how many there were in the packet. I was far more afraid of him than I was of Daisy Wells. I would just have to remember what they said. But how could I remember so many consonants, all jumbled together like nonsense?

As quickly as I could, I clambered up and shoved the box back where I had found it. I listened carefully at the door . . . No noises outside. So I crept thankfully back into the corridor, blinking in the bright light, and slipped into Maxwell's compartment once more. Daisy was not back yet, and I held my breath—had my father noticed that we'd gone? But when I slid the bolt quietly back and pushed open the connecting door a little way, I heard his voice carrying on, threaded through with Maxwell's queries. It was just as though I had never put myself in dreadful peril at all.

It was so strange—the difference between what my father

thought I was doing and my real life—that I had to pop my head round the door and stare in at them. My father looked up over his glasses and gave me a brief, reassuring smile, like a touch on my shoulder. I smiled back, and felt as if I were being pulled in two.

"Hello again, Hazel," he said. He was sitting in a high-backed chair that must have been specially brought in, and Maxwell was on the folded-away bed, taking dictation. "Don't worry. I'll just be a few more minutes and then why don't we all do a crossword together?"

"Yes, Father," I said, hoping desperately that Daisy would come back soon.

Then my father turned back to Maxwell and said, "And the property to be sold . . ."

"And the property to be sold," muttered Maxwell, "currently owned by the aforementioned Mr. Diaz, must be—"

"Auctioned," said my father, "auctioned on the—Apologies, Hazel, I'll be with you soon."

I pulled my head back. Once again, although my father was dealing with money and business and all those complicated things, it seemed as though he were the innocent one, and I the grown-up.

IX

I waited and waited, but Daisy still did not come back. Whatever could she be doing? I became so twitchy that I could hardly stay in my seat. Had she been caught spying? Was she in trouble? Did she need my help?

I decided that I had to act.

"Father!" I called, putting my head round the door once more. "I've ripped my stocking. Can we go and ask Hetty to patch it up?"

My father looked up, concerned.

"We'll be perfectly safe," I said hurriedly. "I promise. We'll come back if even the smallest bit of danger happens."

"Very well, then," said my father. "But be careful, Hazel."

"Yes, Father," I said, hiding a sigh. I knew that I had confused him by looking in on him so many times: he thought I was frightened, instead of spying, but sometimes I think parents don't realize how old you really are, or how much you can do.

"Come on, Daisy!" I said brightly to the empty room, and then I walked out into the corridor, sounding as much like two people as I could.

It was empty again, all the doors closed. Although I could hear dim voices from the dining car, Daisy was not loitering outside, so I turned the other way, trying to guess where she might be. Then I heard a little scuffling noise coming from Mrs. Daunt's compartment.

I crept up to the door, as softly as I could, and inched it open.

"Hello, Watson," whispered Daisy, looking up from where she was kneeling on the floor, over a dark stain that made me shudder. "Come in!"

"How did you know it was me?" I whispered back, wriggling through the gap and pushing the door closed behind me.

"Hmph," she said. "I always know it's you. I would know you out of every person in the universe. You roll your feet out when you walk, and you step with your heel instead of your toe. How did you know it was me?"

"You weren't near the dining car," I said. "And anyway, a grown-up would have been much noisier. I told my father that I'd ripped my stocking, and we were going to visit Hetty to get it fixed. What have you found out?"

"Oh, Il Mysterioso is a dreadful witness," said Daisy, rolling her eyes in the gloom. "All he'll say is that he was alone

Robin Stevens

in his compartment, practicing a new trick, and he was so engrossed that he didn't hear the noise. He's either perfectly innocent or lying through his teeth. It was all becoming very boring, so I thought I'd take the opportunity to investigate the crime scene instead. Did you find the necklace?"

"No," I said. "And no bloodstains, either. I suppose he might have covered himself with something, the way we thought, and then thrown it out of the window after he'd finished killing Mrs. Daunt."

"Indeed," said Daisy. "The only thing that *could* go out of those windows is clothes."

"I found documents, though," I said. "Hidden in a magic box. They look important—I think they must be what he's going to hand over to the Germans!"

Daisy's face brightened with excitement. "Where are they? Show me!"

"I, er, left them," I said guiltily. "I didn't want him to miss them."

"Hazel! You chump! Why ever did you do that? But what did they say?"

I felt worse and worse. "They . . . I think they were in German. I couldn't read them. But there was something that looked like *Character*, and something about *Catholics*."

"Oh, Hazel!" Daisy frowned. "They must be proof that he's the spy. They might even prove that he killed Mrs. Daunt . . . And you left them!"

"Sorry," I whispered. I felt more and more guilty. I really ought to have taken one, but I'd been terrified that Il Mysterioso might realize, and come after us. I imagined him striding toward us, cloak flapping about him like a bat, beard terrible. He would surely not hesitate to hurt us, and if it came out that we knew his secret . . . I shuddered. If he was the murderer we were searching for, as well as the spy, he was our most terrible foe yet.

"Well," said Daisy. "Although you have not behaved as a Detective Society vice president ought, there is still time to redeem yourself. Let's decide on our next steps. As agreed in our Plan of Action, we must find Mrs. Daunt's will to confirm who really does benefit from it."

"But why would she bring it on the train?" I asked. "Surely it's more likely to be in a safe at her house, or in a bank?"

"Well, you never know, do you? She brought the necklace on the train, didn't she? Anyway, there may be something else useful to be discovered. Now, hunt!"

I was not sure—but all the same, I obeyed. Daisy went through Mrs. Daunt's drawers and patted down her dresses, while I lifted down her small attaché case and sifted through the papers in it. After what I had said, I was sure we would not find anything; but then, beneath a deed of sale—with an astonishing number of zeros at the end—and an insurance document for the ruby necklace, I found *The Last Will and Testament of Georgiana Daunt*.

"Daisy!" I whispered. *"It's here after all!"*

Daisy gave a low whistle. "Watson!" she said. "Why, you clever thing! I suppose I can nearly forgive you for leaving behind that crucial evidence before."

I bit my lip and said nothing. We read the will together. It was quite simple, one page only. It had been drawn up only a month ago. There was £2,000 to Mr. Robert Strange "in memory of Mama," £5,000 to Madame Melinda Fox "in gratitude for her help in a difficult time" ("Good Lord!" whispered Daisy, goggling. "That must have been a dreadful lot of help!"), and everything else went to "my beloved husband William Daunt."

We stared at each other. "Well," said Daisy. "Two thousand pounds is enough to commit a murder for, especially if you're hard up. And we know that Mr. Strange is."

I nodded. "So is five thousand, though."

"Yes—if only Mrs. Vitellius hadn't already given Madame Melinda an alibi! What a bother. Still, I think we've found some useful—"

And that was when the door opened again.

X

We stood there, frozen—and through it came Alexander. He was on tiptoe, and when he saw us he jumped.

"What the heck are you doing here?" he hissed.

"What are *you* doing here?" asked Daisy, with great dignity. "We were here first."

"Yes, but . . ." Alexander's eyes narrowed as he looked at us, surrounded by papers. "Wait. Are you *detecting*? You told me you didn't care about crime!"

"We don't!" snapped Daisy. "We're . . . tidying up. Girls tidy up. And I suppose you're here because Dr. Sandwich told you to come?"

"Erm . . ." said Alexander. "Not exactly. He doesn't—precisely—know what I'm doing. He told me to take a break, but I thought I'd just come in here first and . . . check some stuff out."

Suddenly I wanted to laugh. Alexander was doing just

what we were. For all that he was a boy, and American, underneath it all he was *exactly* like us. He was a detective too.

"I know you're detecting," he said. "You can't hide it from me."

"You dare tell!" hissed Daisy.

"I won't tell anyone!" Alexander looked at her anxiously. "After all, you caught me at it too. You could drop me in it just as badly, so I won't say anything if you won't. Pax?"

Daisy pursed her lips and folded her arms. I knew she was about to refuse—and I made a decision. I stepped forward and held out my hand. "Pax," I said. "You're right. We're detecting too."

"Hazel!" cried Daisy, scandalized.

"He can tell us about the interviews," I said. "Oh, Daisy, don't be like that! It'll just be while we're on the train."

"I'll swap you," said Alexander. It was strange, I thought, how I could hear both American and English in his accent all at once. "The interviews for Mrs. Daunt's will."

"How do you know we know about Mrs. Daunt's will?" Daisy asked. "You're making dreadful assumptions."

"Because that's what you were looking at when I came in," he said, raising his eyebrows at us. "Good thick paper, several signatures at the bottom, a lawyer's crest—what else could it be?"

I had to admit that Alexander seemed like a rather good

detective. Daisy scowled, which I knew meant that she had come to the same conclusion.

"All right," she said, the words dragged out of her reluctantly. "Share and share alike. But *only* for this journey. You are not becoming a proper member of the Detective Society."

"That's OK," said Alexander cheerily. "You can't be a member of the Junior Pinkertons either. My friend George would kill me. Now, how d'you want to fix the rest of these interviews?"

Part Four

The Detective Society Practices Some Deception

The dining car was deserted, all the starchy white tables looking quite empty and unloved without their crystal and tableware. According to Alexander, Dr. Sandwich had retreated to his compartment to rest, and Jocelyn had gone to organize the other attendants in the Calais–Athens coach. The interviews would resume at eleven. By my wristwatch, it was five minutes to. We had to hurry.

On one of the tables a notebook lay open, its pages weighed down with black squiggles. I peered at it—I couldn't make head or tail of it.

Alexander translated it for me. "'I was practicing my new trick in my compartment, concentrating so hard that I did not even hear the scream.' Told you I knew shorthand," he said with a grin, and I began to wonder whether I ought to learn, for the good of the Detective Society. "Now, what did that will say?"

"What did Mr. Strange say in his interview?" Daisy countered. She was still acting as though we were at war.

"You first," said Alexander, fiddling with his short cuffs. "Honor bright, I'll tell you after that."

I believed him. "All right," I said, and I explained about the will. I did not mention the spy, though. I did not like to think what Mrs. Vitellius might do to us if we betrayed her and the British government—and I knew that Daisy would be desperate for us to keep at least one piece of information exclusively for the Detective Society.

"Now for mine," said Alexander, once I had finished. "The prints have been wiped off Mr. Strange's knife—it's no good looking for the murderer that way. Mr. Strange keeps on saying that it must have been stolen from his room, but he doesn't know when. And he's awfully muddled about what he did after dinner. He said that he knocked on Mrs. Daunt's door, but she didn't answer—and then he changed his story, and said that he never had. I think the first story's got to be the truth. He's desperate for money—definitely desperate enough to kill Mrs. Daunt for two thousand pounds—but what I want to know, even though it hasn't occurred to Dr. Sandwich, is how he bought a ticket for this train if he's so penniless."

I sat up. This was an extremely good point. How could Mr. Strange afford the Orient Express? Daisy had gone very still, and I knew that she was kicking herself for missing this.

"Mr. Daunt thinks it was Mr. Strange who killed Mrs. Daunt, by the way," Alexander went on. "I can tell. In his interview he kept going on about the knife and how poor Mr. Strange is. He's furious with Madame Melinda, too, for driving Mrs. Daunt out of the dining car. When he went after her, he knocked on her door and she told him to leave her alone. I think he's feeling guilty now, for going back to the dining car and not staying with her.

"Then there's Il Mysterioso. He says he went to his compartment to work on a new trick, and didn't even hear the scream. But I don't see how that could be true—it was so loud! I think he's hiding something."

I thought of the papers I had found in Il Mysterioso's room. But, as I had decided before, this was one piece of information that we could not share with Alexander. "We think the fact that he's a magician is important," I said, to give him something. "After all, the doors were both locked."

"Oh yes," said Alexander. "I've been trying to work that out, but—"

Suddenly we heard Dr. Sandwich's nasal voice outside the dining car. "Ah, Mr. Buri, are you ready to begin the next part of the investigation?"

"Indeed, Dr. Sandwich," said Jocelyn, although he sounded rather tired.

"Excellent, excellent . . ."

I had frozen. Daisy's fists were clenched on the table. We had to hide, otherwise they would come in and see us.

"Quick!" Alexander hissed. "Under the table! They'll never see you down there!"

There was nothing else for it. I dived, bruising my knees and burning my hands on the carpet, and Daisy popped down after me like a rabbit.

O h, hello, Dr. Sandwich, Jocelyn," said Alexander, quite calmly, from above us. I stared at his shiny shoes in a turmoil. Although we were quite hidden by the white starchy fall of the tablecloth around us, I felt as exposed as if I had been served up on a platter. We were trapped like mice in a cage—like the trunk at Deepdean all over again. Daisy butted her head against my shoulder, and I looked round at her in the gloom. She was making a face at me, and wriggling her fingers—it took me a moment to understand that she meant me to take notes. That is Daisy through and through: whatever bind we are in, she has to keep on detecting.

"Hello, Mr. Arcady!" cried Dr. Sandwich, in infuriatingly cheerful tones. "Most excellent. Now our party is back up to strength, and refreshed, I hope—so we move on to our next interview, with the medium Madame Melinda. And here she is now. Come in, come in, madame!"

I heard the beads on Madame Melinda's gown clacking toward us, and then I saw her little buttoned boots gliding across the carpet. They looked very neat and secret under her skirt, and she tucked them under her chair as she sat down. She smelled very strongly of perfume, and Daisy made a disgusted face.

"Madame, it is so kind of you to volunteer your time. Mr. Buri and I will be asking questions, and Mr. Arcady here will be taking notes. At this stage we are merely making preliminary inquiries. Now, before we begin, is there anything you wish to tell us?"

"I should think so!" Madame Melinda's voice was rich and heavy, and her perfume made my nose tickle. "If you ask me, this is all the fault of poor, sweet Georgiana's husband. That man! He was the most dreadful, dangerous influence—one always felt that he was on the verge of doing something really violent. If you're looking for an explanation of what happened last night, I can only suggest that you look to him."

"Madame Melinda," said Dr. Sandwich reasonably, "that is all very well, but you must know that Mr. Daunt is quite above suspicion. Why, he was in the dining car, in the company of several other guests and attendants, when Mrs. Daunt screamed."

"Well, on a physical level he was," said Madame Melinda darkly, "but *spiritually* he was up to no good. He is a wicked

Robin Stevens

presence. Why, I have never met a person so able to darken the mood of a room. Even if he had not been so patently unsupportive of my séances, I would have had to banish him from them. You mark my words, whichever hand held the knife, Mr. Daunt was spurring them on."

"Thank you, madame," said Dr. Sandwich. "Now, it would be helpful if you could give us an account of your relationship with Mrs. Daunt—how did you meet, and what was the nature of your friendship?"

"Dear Georgiana contacted me after the death of her beloved mother last year. She wanted to use me to contact the Other Side, and I am glad to say that the spirits were willing. We had some touching séances—truly touching—and I feel that I helped both mother and daughter accept their new situation. Mr. Daunt, though, had the nerve to accuse me of being a charlatan. Me! Why, even as a very young child I saw faces and heard voices, and as I have matured—"

"Thank you, Madame Melinda," interrupted Dr. Sandwich. "Quite fascinating, I'm sure. What can you tell me about the events of last night?"

"It is quite simple. I left the dining car in the company of the lady from compartment seven, next door to my own— Mrs. Vitellius. We parted at the door, and then I sat at my dresser and began my toilette. I could hear people moving about in the compartments on either side, and that was when I was simply overcome with a communication from the Other Side. It's so dreadful to think, isn't it, that I must have heard Mrs. Daunt's killer enter the room? If only I had been paying attention . . . Of course, the communication was a premonition of Georgie's death, but I had no time to understand the message properly. Then Mrs. Vitellius rapped on our connecting wall for some reason—and the very next moment, poor Georgie screamed!"

I nudged Daisy. There, laid out for us, was the corroboration of Mrs. Vitellius's statement. She had knocked to tell Madame Melinda to be quiet, and Madame Melinda had heard—that placed them both in their rooms at the crucial moment, and thus above suspicion. We had ruled out two suspects!

"Can you remember anything of what you heard from Mrs. Daunt's room?" urged Dr. Sandwich. "Anything at all? A . . . male voice, perhaps? Heavy shoes that could not have belonged to Mrs. Daunt herself?"

Under the table I sat up, frowning. Daisy has taught me that it is important not to ask leading questions.

"A male voice?" asked Madame Melinda. "Oh—well . . . it could have been. I cannot deny it, certainly. I was in such a state, but . . . well, there was certainly *someone* in the room with her. But you mustn't take my word for it! Why, you can ask Mrs. Daunt herself!"

I heard an exclamation from Jocelyn, and Dr. Sandwich said, "Whatever do you mean?"

Robin Stevens

"I plan to hold a séance this evening," said Madame Melinda, as though it was as ordinary as holding a tea party. "If the spirit of Georgiana has passed over to the Other Side, I will be able to contact her and hear the true story of last night's events. I wish to help you bring her murderer to justice!"

"Madame Melinda!" said Jocelyn, sounding rather faint. "Our other guests . . . please, the disruption—"

"No, no, Mr. Buri, wait!" said Dr. Sandwich. "Think. Is this not a marvellous opportunity to get at the truth? Whether or not one believes in the spirit world (I am sure that there is room for both science and mystery), this will bring all our suspects together, and who knows what secrets may come out? Madame Melinda, you have our full approval in this endeavor. If you will allow us to sit with you, and watch—why, we may have this case wrapped up before the train reaches Belgrade!"

"Of course you may," said Madame Melinda. "Your energies are positive. Yes, I think you will contribute nicely to the evening. May I leave?"

"Indeed, indeed," said Dr. Sandwich. "That will be all for now, thank you."

I could tell that, mentally, he had already moved on, but I wanted to hear more about this séance—where did Madame Melinda mean to hold it? Would we be allowed to be there? Was she really going to contact Mrs. Daunt?

I felt creepy when I imagined it. And, I thought suddenly, Dr. Sandwich had forgotten to ask Madame Melinda what she had seen when she reached Mrs. Daunt's compartment after the scream. What if she had some crucial piece of evidence? But Madame Melinda's little button-shoed feet were already moving past my nose, in small, precise, rolling steps, and then she was out of the door and away.

"The Countess next," said Dr. Sandwich.

A h," said Dr. Sandwich above me. "Good morning, my lady."

"Good morning, Dr. Sandwich, Mr. Buri, Alexander," said the Countess, and her feet—and her elegant little cane—stumped over to our table. I had a momentary vision of the cane shooting out to poke us, revealing our hiding place to the world, but she leaned it against her chair.

"Ought my grandson to be present at this interview?" asked the Countess. "It seems highly irregular. Why, you have no way of being sure that he won't alter my answers to protect me!"

"*Grandmother!*" said Alexander.

"So you believe you need protecting?" asked Dr. Sandwich quickly.

"Certainly not," she retorted, her voice sharp. "It was merely my joke. Surely you can recognize a joke when you hear one, Dr. Sandwich?"

She said his name in a way that showed me she was utterly scornful of everything to do with him.

"I have been told that I have an excellent sense of humor," said Dr. Sandwich. "Although I am not one to boast. Now, tell us about what happened at dinner—anything that you can still remember."

"If you please, my lady," added Jocelyn. He at least could see that Dr. Sandwich was setting the Countess's teeth on edge.

"Dinner," she replied coldly. Jocelyn had not appeased her in the slightest. "Well. Now, I am an old and feeble woman, but I can still remember the events of the evening before, if I try very hard. Dinner . . . it was soup, was it not, followed by chicken and fish? And then crêpes—but I never eat sweet things. They are bad for my digestion. That common man who stole my necklace had a falling-out with his wife, and then an argument with that fool who pretends to be able to speak to ghosts. Alexander and I ignored them, of course."

She was obviously trying her hardest not to say anything important at all. In the half-dark I could see Daisy grinning admiringly.

"Why do you say that it was *your* necklace, my lady?"

"Because it is!" said the Countess sharply. "Alexander, stop writhing about like that. Alexander does not understand *moral* ownership, you see. He is too modern. Our family may have had to sell the jewel to pay for passage to England after the troubles in Russia, but it is a part of us, and a part of us it shall always remain. I told Mrs. Daunt so last night."

"When?" asked Dr. Sandwich eagerly.

"How should I remember?" snapped the Countess. "I said it several times."

Jocelyn cleared his throat.

Dr. Sandwich went on, "But after dinner—did you speak to Mrs. Daunt about the necklace *after* dinner?"

"You expect me to recall that?" asked the Countess. "I am an old, infirm woman—quite near death."

I had never met an old person who was so obviously *not* infirm. Her voice was sharp and clear and her brain was spinning far faster than Dr. Sandwich's.

The Countess must remember getting up after dinner, saying that she was going to speak to Mrs. Daunt. I certainly did. And judging by the way Alexander's foot tapped against the table leg, he remembered as well. Had she found her? Had they argued, and had something dreadful happened? Was that why the necklace was missing?

"So when you heard the scream, you were—"

"In my compartment," said the Countess coldly. "Quite alone, and quite innocent. I heard the scream, I stood up—rather slowly, as I am getting on in years; I need this cane—and went limping out into the corridor to find the other guests already there. Once Mr. Daunt had broken down the door, I looked inside and saw the body—and noticed that the necklace was missing."

Was it true that she could not walk without her cane? I wondered. If so, it would be a point in her favor. After all, we knew that the murderer must have moved fearfully quickly to escape from the compartment before we appeared in the corridor. But after not saying why she had left the dining car last night, I was not sure whether I could trust anything the Countess said.

"Yes, the necklace may be an important clue," said Dr. Sandwich.

"A clue!" cried the Countess. "It is the most important part of this case!"

"Come now, my lady . . ." He cleared his throat like he was teaching a lesson. "We are dealing in murder! There is no crime more serious that one man can commit against another. Theft, though important *in its way*, cannot be compared to the loss of a human life."

"You, Dr. Sandwich, have obviously never owned a truly excellent stone," said the Countess sharply. "Jewels mean something, and their loss is to be mourned. Do not despise what you cannot understand."

I wanted him to press her—did she have a hand in the theft of the necklace? And was that connected to the murder? But he only said, "Thank you, my lady, that will be all." My fingers were itching—Dr. Sandwich could not be trusted to do anything properly.

And then, from the corridor outside, we heard a knock. I thought one of the passengers must be knocking on a compartment door—but then I heard a pattern to it; a pattern that spelled out S-O-S. There was only one other person on the train who would contact us using Morse code. It had to be Hetty. And if she was trying to alert us covertly—well, it could only mean one thing: if we did not get out of the dining car soon, Daisy and I would be in very serious trouble indeed.

I clutched Daisy's arm in panic. She sat hunched up, her face tense. Hetty had given the danger signal, we both knew that—but what were we to do? I ought to have been used to this sort of thing by now—most of Daisy's ideas are dangerous: all or nothing; jumping off the ledge and hoping that there is something to land on. But I was still terrified. I clenched my fists in despair.

"You may go, my lady, thank you," said Dr. Sandwich, from above me. I only heard him dimly, my mind was whirring so hard. Could we crawl out after the Countess? But how could we get all the way to the door without anyone noticing two little (or not so little) girls wriggling across the carpet? I decided that, for all they were glamorous, and served glorious food, I disliked trains. There was nowhere to *creep* in them—it was out in the open or nothing.

"Grandmother," said Alexander. "Here, let me help you to the door. It isn't so very far."

I was confused by his contradiction, but then his shoe nudged my hand, and I realized what he was doing. He had heard the code as well, and was helping fellow detectives in trouble. I decided that we had been quite right to confide in him.

The Countess stood up, leaning on her cane. After her went Alexander, and after them we had to go.

Out from under the table I crawled, on my elbows and knees, shuffling across the carpet, and Daisy followed like a snake. She even crawls gracefully. I was terrified that Jocelyn or Dr. Sandwich would look down and see us—but thankfully, they did not.

"Alexander," whispered the Countess above me, and I hoped like anything that she was looking up at him as she said it. "Listen, I want you to promise me . . . Really, bend down—it isn't reasonable of children to *grow* the way you do! It's up to you to look after the family honor. If they try to search my compartment . . . You know what a shock that would be to me. You mustn't let them."

"Grandmother!" said Alexander, lowering his voice too so that Dr. Sandwich could not hear. "You haven't done anything, have you?"

"Don't ask questions!" she snapped. "Just remember what I said. Don't disappoint me. Now, let go of my arm. I can manage perfectly well on my own."

I saw her stand up straighter—she seemed to be barely

leaning on her cane. *Was* she telling the truth about needing it to walk?

The doorway was in front of me. We were nearly there. Feeling desperately daring, I gripped this casebook between my teeth and pitched forward once again, the thick pile of the carpet rubbing against my hands and knees.

With the Countess stalking ahead, mercifully not looking down, we went out into the corridor. I rolled and almost bumped into Hetty, who was leaning against the wall. Daisy got to her feet, and then, from halfway down the corridor, there was a shout.

"HAZEL WONG! WHAT are you doing crawling about on the floor like a worm?"

I was on my feet so quickly that it made me dizzy. Ahead of me, I noticed, the Countess had hunched back over her cane, the very image of a helpless old lady.

My father was striding toward me, a most unimpressed expression on his face.

"I was . . ." I said. "We were . . . playing a game."

"Hazel! You are not six years old any longer! Really, this is all deeply . . . unladylike!"

"Terribly sorry, Mr. Wong!" said Daisy cheerfully. "Hazel and I were pretending to be Melusine, you see, and she hasn't any legs."

"In front of these people?" asked my father, gesturing at

186   *Robin Stevens*

the Countess and Alexander, who had stopped and turned to look at us.

I wanted to curl up in a ball and hide. It was dreadfully embarrassing.

"Children will be children," said the Countess. "I never seem to know what my grandson is getting up to these days. Pretending to be a detective—hah!"

My father shot me a very suspicious look. I shook my head desperately.

"You, girl!" said the Countess suddenly, glaring at Daisy. "You're Lord Hastings's child, aren't you?"

Daisy's chin went up. "Yes, my lady," she said.

"Terrible trouble, that," said the Countess. "You know, I often think that it's important for dreadful things to happen to you. It makes you more of a person. But it's important to stand up to them—not wriggle about on the floor in distress. Remember that."

"Thank you, my lady," said Daisy—and I heard in her voice that she really meant it.

Then the Countess turned and disappeared into her compartment.

y father was most confused. He was desperate to accuse us of breaking the rules he had laid down—but apart from some very unmannerly wriggling on the carpet, he could not see exactly what we had done wrong.

"It really is strange of you, Hazel," he told me. "Why can't you be a leader? You ought to be showing Miss Wells how to behave. Now, I want the two of you to come and sit quietly in Maxwell's compartment until lunch and do a crossword puzzle—use your brains properly."

"Yes, Father," I said. "I'm sorry, Father."

"That's my good girl," said my father, and patted me on the head as if I were still a shrimp.

So back we went to Maxwell's compartment—I was thoroughly sick of it by now—and I put this casebook back on my lap and scribbled away in it. We had narrowed the suspects down to four—Il Mysterioso, Mr. Strange, Sarah, and the Countess.

I reflected, not for the first time, how very unusual my life was. We were on the Orient Express, discussing spies and murder and theft—and it was *not* our imagination, but hard, cold facts. I had seen the body, and I had read the letter proving that Mrs. Vitellius really was on the trail of a dangerous spy. But there is truth, and then there is what is believable, and I knew that we could not stop until we had every link in the chain ready to wrap around our murderer and our spy (or both, if Il Mysterioso were guilty).

But what if the murderer realized that we suspected them? This had been worrying me. If they came after us, we should have nowhere to hide. Our only disguise was who we were—which also meant that we could not announce our suspicions until we were absolutely sure. It was true that we were both detectives and schoolgirls, but it was not likely. And unless we could narrow our four suspects down further, we would never be believed.

I wrote in my casebook:

Perhaps Madame Melinda's seance will help.

Daisy, looking indignant, replied immediately:

Seances! Hazel, really, you must stop believing in ghosts!

I don't! But she does. And she might frighten whoever did it into believing too. Anyway, you can't get on your high horse. Remember the Ouija board!

Daisy had cleverly—although rather creepily—used a Ouija board during our first murder investigation, and it had been extremely effective.

Daisy huffed.

That was quite different. But you may have a point. We must keep watch. Constant vigilance!

"Daisy? Hazel?" said my father from next door. "How are you, girls?"

"Very well, Mr. Wong!" Daisy called back, winking at me. "We've just solved a rather important clue. Ten down: *innocence*. The puzzle is beginning to fall into place."

SUSPECT LIST

Mr. Strange. MOTIVE: He is Mrs. Daunt's brother, and did not get any money from their mother's will. She got everything. He does not seem to be making any money from his books either. Therefore he might have killed Mrs. Daunt because he hoped to get something

Robin Stevens

from her will; or he might have killed her out of spite at having been overlooked, or jealousy. NOTES: His knife was the murder weapon. He said it was stolen—is this true? He was in the sleeping car at the moment when Mrs. Daunt screamed. He writes crime novels—is this suspicious? He says he did not know that the Daunts would be on the train—is this true?

We know that he gains £2,000 from Mrs. Daunt's will—enough to make the murder seem worthwhile. How did he pay for his journey on the Orient Express? We must investigate.

The Countess. MOTIVE: She believes that Mrs. Daunt's ruby necklace is really hers. The necklace is now missing. Did she kill Mrs. Daunt to steal it? NOTES: She was in the sleeping car at the moment when Mrs. Daunt screamed.

She is hiding the fact that she left the dining car to speak to Mrs. Daunt from Dr. Sandwich. Is it true that she can only walk with a cane, or is she just pretending?

Il Mysterioso. MOTIVE: We believe that he is the spy Mrs. Vitellius is investigating. Did Mrs. Daunt discover his secret, forcing him to silence her? NOTES:

He was in the sleeping car at the moment when Mrs. Daunt screamed, but he did not appear in the corridor when Mrs. Daunt's body was discovered, despite the noise. Why did he stay in his compartment?

And he is a magician—who else would be able to perform a locked-room trick so well? He is clearly hiding something from Dr. Sandwich. We found suspicious papers in his compartment, but do not know what they say. We must find out.

Madame Melinda. MOTIVE: ~~We know that Mrs. Daunt was paying her to contact her dead mother, and Mr. Daunt did not like it. He was trying to get his wife away from Madame Melinda—Madame Melinda can't have wanted to lose Mrs. Daunt's money. Might she have thought that she would gain from Mrs. Daunt's will?~~ NOTES: ~~She was in the sleeping car at the moment when Mrs Daunt screamed. She also used to be an actress—Il Mysterioso said so—so she must be very good at pretending.~~ RULED OUT: Mrs. Vitellius left the dining car with her, and heard her in her compartment at the moment of the scream.

Sarah. MOTIVE: She seemed to dislike Mrs. Daunt. We know from Hetty that she was stealing from her, and we saw her threatening to give in her notice. But is unhappiness with her job enough to make her kill her mistress? Or did Mrs. Daunt find out about the thefts and threaten to hand her over to the police? NOTES: She was in the sleeping car at the moment when Mrs. Daunt screamed.

Sarah is still a mystery to us—we must investigate her further!

Mrs. Vitellius. ~~MOTIVE: None that we can see yet. But we know that she is not who others believe her to be. She was also in the sleeping car at the moment when Mrs. Daunt screamed.~~ RULED OUT: She left the dining car with Madame Melinda and was heard in her compartment by her just before the scream.

L unch was a very subdued affair. Mrs. Vitellius picked at her food, Madame Melinda wrung her hands and glared at Mr. Daunt, who sat hunched over his plate, his eyes bloodshot, and Mr. Strange scribbled on another bit of paper, glancing guiltily about the room. Il Mysterioso was not even trying to eat. He had pushed his pork loin away from him, as though it offended him, and was glaring at it. I felt my father's eyes on Daisy and me at every moment—and it did not help that Daisy was seething at the fact that the interviews were over and we had not even been questioned.

"Dr. Sandwich has dreadfully poor judgment," she whispered as she took a bite of pork. I quite agreed; I felt indignant as well. Although my father and Maxwell had been questioned about what they had seen and heard at dinner the previous day, Dr. Sandwich had not spoken to me or Daisy. He did not know what he was doing, and I had no faith that he would be able to solve such a complicated murder. I had found out from Hetty that he had not spoken to the servants either, which was very shortsighted of him. Daisy and I knew from the mystery at Fallingford that servants often observe more than anybody else.

Of course, Hetty didn't know anything about the murder—she had been with us in the dining car—but Sarah was different. I saw that Hetty was speaking to her, but Sarah was ignoring her and watching Mr. Daunt. She was not looking at him in the same hateful way I had seen earlier, either—was this important?

Just then, Daisy went quite still. I looked at her questioningly, and she mouthed, *"Listen!"*

And as soon as I listened, I understood. There were noises coming from the corridor—muffled thumps and bangs; doors opening and closing. Every time I think I have learned to notice everything, Daisy reminds me that, compared to her, I am really quite blinkered. Of course, the attendants were searching our rooms while we were having lunch. But what would they find?

The thumpings grew louder, and now some of the other passengers heard them as well.

"Excuse me!" said the Countess, sitting up in alarm. "Excuse me! What is that noise?"

One of the waiters, seeing her unhappy face, slipped out, and came back with Jocelyn. He stood in the doorway and cleared his throat.

"Ladies and gentlemen," he said. "If I may have your attention for a moment . . . There is no cause for alarm, but I must inform you that we are currently searching your compartments."

The Countess gasped. She stood up, leaning heavily on her cane. "How DARE you?" she cried. "Don't you know who I am? Why, if we were in Russia, I should have you whipped!"

"We are conducting a murder investigation, my lady," said Jocelyn apologetically. "If you remember, I asked you not to lock your doors today—this is why."

"This," said Madame Melinda loudly, puffing herself out until she seemed to fill the room with indignation and black taffeta, "is a breach of privacy. It is quite ridiculous."

"Are you trying to interfere with the investigation into my wife's murder?" bellowed Mr. Daunt, glaring at her. His stained napkin from lunch was balled up in his fist, and he looked as if he wanted to crush Madame Melinda in exactly the same way.

Mr. Strange was white-faced and the Countess was trembling, but neither of them looked as terrified as Il Mysterioso. He was shaking all over—and when I turned toward the doorway, I saw what had upset him. Dr. Sandwich had appeared, and in his hands was the magic box I had discovered that morning.

"Aha!" he cried. "Observe—a clue!"

Robin Stevens

I could tell at once that, as far as Il Mysterioso was concerned, nothing worse could have happened.

"That is a magical prop," he said shakily, his Italian accent stronger than ever. "That is from my private collection—private, I tell you—as a magician, I must be allowed certain secrets."

"Quiet, sir," snapped Dr. Sandwich. "Sit down at this chair and open it at once, or I shall arrest you for murder."

"He can't do that!" hissed Daisy in my ear. "Who does he think he is?"

Il Mysterioso began to sit—and then he bucked upright and made a dive for the door. Jocelyn sprang across to stop him, and two waiters pinned him firmly against the wall, making the cutlery rattle.

"*Sit down,*" said Dr. Sandwich, clearly enjoying the drama terribly, "*and open this box.*"

"You'll have to smash it first," said Il Mysterioso.

There was a clicking noise and he flung his arms upward; when he swept his cloak back, we all saw that he had attached his wrists to the metal luggage rack above the tables with two heavy silver chains. It was a most excellent magic trick—I couldn't help gasping.

The Countess clapped her little gloved hands together, and for a moment she stood up straight, her cane forgotten. Madame Melinda made a noise rather like a snort, and Mr. Daunt growled.

"Jocelyn," said Dr. Sandwich, pursing his lips, "fetch some bolt cutters immediately."

My father got to his feet, looking very neat and ordered. "Excuse me," he said, "but I believe I can be of assistance."

"*You?*" said Mr. Daunt. "What are you going to do, Fu Manchu—magic it open?"

I flinched, and my cheeks burned with horror, but my father has had years more than I have to learn calm. I told myself that it did not matter if most people in the West could not see him properly. He was still kinder, and cleverer, than all the other grown-up passengers on this Orient Express put together. But all the same, I wished that I were not the only one who knew it.

"Alas, I have no more magical powers than anyone in this carriage," my father said politely—which was a very neat hidden dig at Il Mysterioso and Madame Melinda.

My father has no time for mystery and magic. Everything

Robin Stevens

must be logical and measurable. I am very glad he never knew about our seventh-grade Spiritualist Society. "However, I do know the trick of these boxes. They are all built along the same lines, you see. If I may . . . ?"

After a pause Dr. Sandwich grudgingly motioned him toward the box. "But no funny business, do you hear me?"

"None," said my father, and only I (and perhaps Daisy) detected an edge to his voice. He sat down at the table across from Il Mysterioso, his square, sensible hands in full view, and began to run them across the box's surface, tracing its leaves and flowers and half-hidden birds. Even faster than I had, he made it click and spring open, and the papers spilled across the tabletop.

Geburtstag, I read once again. *Katholisch*. What did it mean?

My father quickly shuffled through them, his eyes taking everything in. Would he be able to explain the mystery?

"These appear to be birth certificates," he said mildly, looking up at Il Mysterioso. "How did they come to be in your possession?"

"Excuse me, I am in charge of this investigation, and I shall be asking the questions," said Dr. Sandwich, nose bulging with excitement. "You! How did these birth certificates get into this box?"

"I put them there, naturally," said Il Mysterioso, and despite his fear I could hear a sudden hint of mocking laughter in his voice.

"But why? What is all this? Explain yourself at *once*."

"They are my family's birth certificates," said Il Mysterioso. "As a good Catholic, I naturally have many family members."

"*Good Catholic!*" cried the Countess dismissively. "Nonsense. You're a Jew!"

Dr. Sandwich sat up in great excitement. "Jewish?" he cried. "Are you sure?"

"Of course I am!" said the Countess firmly. "I suspected as much, but I saw the truth at lunch today. He didn't touch his pork."

"Hah!" said Dr. Sandwich, his eyes lighting up. He turned to Il Mysterioso. "And I'll be bound these are forged documents that you are smuggling across Europe. Mrs. Daunt discovered your game, didn't she? She was going to alert the authorities, and so you had to kill her to keep your secret!"

"Jews can't be trusted," the Countess announced. "Don't you know they all hoard money?"

"Grandmother!" cried Alexander, horrified. "You *can't* say things like that. It isn't true."

"It certainly is not. And I have never murdered anyone!" said Il Mysterioso. "Those papers have nothing to do with the murder. Last night I left the dining car to work on a new piece of magic. When I work, I am lost to the world— that is why I did not hear the scream at once."

Robin Stevens

"Unlikely," said Dr. Sandwich. "And what magic trick do you claim to have been working on?"

"A . . . a locked-room escape," said Il Mysterioso.

"Hah! Mrs. Daunt's doors were both locked, as you well know. I have been wondering how the murderer managed it—but a trained magician would have no trouble at all. You went into her room, you cut her throat and you ran out again, locking the door behind you with some cunning trick. I would have asked these attendants to put you in handcuffs, but you have saved me the trouble. All that remains is to discover where you have hidden Mrs. Daunt's necklace, and the mystery will be solved. Ladies, gentlemen, you have nothing to fear. We have found Mrs. Daunt's murderer, and this investigation is over!"

VIII

Excuse me . . ." One of the other attendants was standing in the doorway, a worried expression on his face. "Sir, excuse me."

Jocelyn looked up, and then hurried over, and they whispered together, looking oddly similar in their blue jackets, with their hair neatly clipped against their necks.

"You shall be confined to a compartment of the guards' van—constantly watched, of course. We don't want you escaping!" said Dr. Sandwich, chuckling at his own joke. He rubbed his hands together, and I felt ill.

Everything was going wrong. This was not rigorous, it was not fair, and it was not finished. We did not understand what the documents in Il Mysterioso's magic box meant. They must be evidence of his spying—I looked over at Mrs. Vitellius and saw her covertly watching him—but were they evidence of murder as well? We had not *proved* that Il Mysterioso had been in Mrs. Daunt's compartment at the moment she screamed. And we had not proved that Mrs. Daunt had discovered his secret and threatened to expose him. Yes, he *could* certainly be the murderer, and he could certainly have accomplished the locked-room trick—but we did not *know*, and that made all my detective senses tingle uncomfortably.

"Dr. Sandwich," said Jocelyn. "If I might have a moment—"

"Anything you say to me you can say to the other passengers," said Dr. Sandwich grandly. "We have no secrets any more, after all! The thing is solved!"

"If I could just—"

"Spit it out, man!"

Jocelyn frowned. "Dr. Sandwich," he said, "Raoul has told me something. He was the attendant who turned down the compartments last night after the . . . incident with Mrs. Daunt. Il Mysterioso's door was locked, and as there was no noise he opened it with his master key, and—"

Il Mysterioso writhed. "No!" he cried. "Please!"

"And inside he found Il Mysterioso. Dr. Sandwich, he tells me that the magician was . . . in difficulties."

"*Please!*" cried Il Mysterioso again. Everyone in the dining car was staring from him to Jocelyn in utter confusion. What was going on?

"Raoul says that he was lying on the carpet, chained from hand to foot, and attached to the luggage rack. He seemed to be in great pain, and had clearly been struggling to free himself for some considerable time—an hour, at least. He had to ask Raoul to fetch the key, which was stored in one of the drawers. He told him that he had become entangled while practicing his new magic trick."

"I deny this utterly!" cried Il Mysterioso. "It is a lie! I was working on my trick—that was why I did not come out when I heard the scream. I was never trapped—I did not—"

"But, sir," said Jocelyn, "if this is true, you have an alibi for the time of the crime!"

Was it true? I wondered. Could it be? If Il Mysterioso was a magician, couldn't he have simply *pretended* to be stuck, to create a false alibi? But I looked at Il Mysterioso's face, furious and ashamed, nearly in tears, and somehow I believed it. It was the answer to the question of why he did not come out into the corridor when Mrs. Daunt screamed: because he could not. And he could not explain why without ruining his reputation as a magician.

"Nonsense!" said Dr. Sandwich, but he sounded panicked. "The man's a magician—he must have been pretending—"

"Sir, I am sure he was not," said Raoul, rather shyly. "I apologize—I *have* to speak now, even though the gentleman begged me not to. He told me he would pay me—"

"Oh God," said Il Mysterioso, slumping so that the handcuffs cut into his wrists. It looked dreadfully painful, and I winced. "I'm finished. No new trick for years, and now stuck performing a simple stunt like that! I shall be a laughing stock."

"So . . . you"—Dr Sandwich was almost spitting, like a bubbling pot—"you *didn't do it?*"

"I told you, I was developing a new trick! It went . . . wrong."

"And you would have preferred to be arrested for murder?" cried Jocelyn. "Sir!"

"I didn't do it!" shouted Il Mysterioso. "And those papers—they have nothing to do with anything. Why can't you leave me in peace?"

"I can't believe it!" whispered Daisy. "Oh, this is glorious!"

I knew she meant Dr. Sandwich's embarrassment in front of all the passengers. That *was* quite wonderful—but in ruling out our best suspect, the mystery was wide open once again. Il Mysterioso might still be the spy, but judging from Raoul's evidence, he could not be the murderer. So who else could it be?

IX

But the revelations were not over yet. Another attendant came into the dining car, clutching something in his hand.

"What is this?" cried Dr. Sandwich, struggling to regain control of the situation.

"Pardon me, Dr. Sandwich," said the attendant. "We have discovered something in Mr. Strange's compartment."

He held out his hand. From it dangled something that had once been white, but was now smeared with thick, rusty brown stains. It looked like a large handkerchief.

Mr. Strange froze.

"Is that *blood?*" asked Mrs. Vitellius faintly.

"That isn't mine," said Mr. Strange, getting up in a hurry. "I've never seen it before. I don't know what . . . In my room, you say?"

"In his suitcase, Dr. Sandwich," said the attendant apologetically. "We have also discovered some, er, bits of paper covered in writing. These notes—they all concern the stabbing of a young woman. Mr. Buri, Dr. Sandwich, we felt sure that they were relevant to the case."

"I am a crime writer!" said Mr. Strange. "Those are plans for my next novel—it is to feature a murder on a train. They're not *real*." It was the worst answer he could have given.

"Arrest him!" cried Mr. Daunt, swinging his heavy hand at Mr. Strange.

I saw Dr. Sandwich's face contorting—it was almost funny, watching his certainty flaking away like nibbled pastry. I could tell that Daisy was enjoying it most awfully as well, although of course her face gave nothing away apart from appropriate horror.

Mr. Strange was trembling. "Don't you dare!" he gulped. "I'll . . . You shan't be able to hold me. You'll see—when the police arrive they'll let me go!"

"Take him to the guards' van!" said Dr. Sandwich. "Away from the body, mind. And I want his room searched again! We will get to the bottom of this."

"Ladies and gentlemen!" said Jocelyn as Mr. Strange was led away, and two attendants rushed to fetch bolt cutters to free Il Mysterioso. "*Please!* Sit down, please—finish your meal . . ."

There was a general outcry. Madame Melinda began to shout about Georgiana and the séance, and Jocelyn, looking absolutely exhausted, began to direct and organize, a wagon-lit attendant on each side of him. Alexander looked as though he wanted to come and speak to us, but my father was hovering protectively and he could not get close.

"Mr. Daunt, Mr. Daunt," said Sarah, getting up and hurrying over to Mr. Daunt's table. "Are you quite all right?"

"Do go away, Sarah. Can't you be *quiet?*" he snapped at her.

Sarah stepped back, a shocked look on her face, and then turned and stormed out of the dining car.

"Servants can be so difficult," said the Countess. "Alexander, I feel faint. I need you to help me back to my room. My cane will not suffice."

As Alexander walked past our table, I glanced up at him and he gave me a little smile. I smiled back—but I was wondering again about the Countess. How frail was she, really? Her weakness seemed to come and go as needed.

My father leaned over to me and Daisy. He looked very stern, and I wobbled a bit—I knew he was not cross with us, but all the same I felt his anger against my chest, like a battering ram. "From now on I want you to stay with a grown-up at all times," he said. "This whole thing is being managed dreadfully—how are we to be sure that the murderer has been apprehended? Shocking, putting a man like that in charge!" He glowered at Dr. Sandwich.

"Can we go and sit in Hetty's compartment?" asked Daisy

Robin Stevens

brightly. "I'd feel safer there, away from all this."

I guessed what she was doing. She wasn't worried about our safety. She was making sure we were as close as possible to the one suspect we had still not investigated properly: Sarah.

"Very well," said my father. "You may go to Hetty's compartment. I will speak to her now, and tell her to watch over you. I must say, Miss Wells, that this is a very sensible suggestion. I'm pleased. Perhaps my daughter has been making an impression on you after all . . ."

"Hazel's caution is rubbing off on me," agreed Daisy. "That must be it."

I narrowed my eyes at her. Really, she was laying it on frightfully thick. But my father was too distracted to see it.

"Come on, Hazel," she went on, winking at me quite outrageously. "Let's go and be safe."

X

When we reached Hetty and Sarah's compartment, it was empty. Hetty, of course, was still in the restaurant car speaking to my father, but where was Sarah? The window was shut, and the room was dark and close. I wriggled uncomfortably. "Daisy," I said, "what are we doing?"

"The same as always," she said, rolling her eyes. "Investigating, of course. Anyway, it's not as if we're not supposed to be here. Hetty's *our* maid, after all. Now, quick—before anyone comes in, let's start looking—"

But we had no time to look for anything. With a thump, the door burst open. "Sarah," boomed Mr. Daunt, "follow me—I need to speak to you . . ."

And through the door they both came. But as soon as they were inside Sarah's arms went around his neck, and he bent his face to hers, his nasty moustache rubbing against her mouth.

They were *kissing.*

We stood there, frozen in amazement. Then Mr. Daunt saw us and jumped away from Sarah with a yell. Sarah screamed.

"What are you DOING in here?" Mr. Daunt bellowed at us.

"We were waiting for Hetty!" gasped Daisy, all shocked innocence. You would think she had never seen anything scandalous before in her life. "What were you—Oh!"

"I was giving Sarah her orders," growled Mr. Daunt. "Whatever you thought you saw—you saw nothing, d'you hear?"

"Yes, sir," I whispered. At that moment I was quite simply afraid. Mr. Daunt was so fierce! And was this the motive we had been looking for, for Sarah? It had not made sense for her to have murdered Mrs. Daunt merely because she hated her—but if she was in love with Mr. Daunt, everything was suddenly quite understandable. I was only shocked at Mr. Daunt: he had loved his wife, and here he was, less than a day after she had been murdered, kissing someone else. I suppose grief makes people do odd things.

"You! Fix this!" Mr. Daunt snapped at Sarah, then stormed out without another word.

"Nosy children!" snapped Sarah. "If you say anything, I shall—"

But we never heard what she would do, because at that

moment Hetty came in, gasping and saying, "Oh, isn't this dreadful?"

For a moment I thought she meant Sarah and Mr. Daunt—but of course she only meant Mr. Strange's arrest.

Sarah snapped her mouth shut, sat down and pulled out some mending—one of Mr. Daunt's jackets. She began to sew a button back on it, her fingers jerking the needle through viciously, like someone tightening a noose, and then biting off the thread with her teeth, lip curled and angry. I could see that she wanted to do the same to us. I wondered again why Dr. Sandwich had not thought to question Sarah and Hetty. Of course, in crime novels the servants are not proper characters, but in real life they are. They fall in love, and hate people, just like anyone else. Sarah could just as easily be the murderer as the Countess or Mr. Strange.

"Girls, perhaps this is not the best place for you," said Hetty to us, looking at Sarah. "Shall we go out for a . . . a walk?"

I nodded frantically. I felt a grateful swell in my heart toward Hetty. I loved the red frizz of her hair and the thin bones of her wrists, and I could have hugged her then and there, if that had been the proper English thing to do.

Down the corridor we walked, and I ought to have felt relieved to be out of that compartment, but instead it was as if the train itself were closing in on me. There was danger all around—and until the murder was solved we could not be safe. "I want to go outside properly," I said suddenly.

"Do you think that's a good idea?" asked Hetty. "Not that I wouldn't like to, but your father . . . the bomb, Miss Hazel."

"Oh no, let's!" said Daisy. "It'll make such a lovely change!"

Suddenly Alexander emerged from the Countess's compartment. He looked nervous—I could see that something had upset him.

"Excuse me," he said. "If you're going outside, may I come with you?"

Daisy frowned. "I'm not sure if that's a good idea," she said. "After all, you are a strange man, and we oughtn't to go walking with strange men."

"I'm not a strange man!" said Alexander. "I'm me! Please say yes." I could see that this really mattered to him—although I could not understand why.

"Really, Daisy!" said Hetty. "Manners! If Miss Hazel's father agrees, Master Arcady, of course you may come." She turned away, and quick as a flash Alexander leaned over to us. "You've got to help me!" he whispered. "Something's happened!"

Part Five
On the Right Track

Mr. Wong!" called Hetty.

My father popped his head out into the corridor, glasses tilting down his nose. "What's all this?" he asked. "Hazel, why are you back so soon?"

"The girls and Master Arcady would like to go for a walk outside, sir," said Hetty, "But . . . well . . ."

My father was staring down at me as though he could burrow straight inside my head and see every bad thought there. "Are you sure?" he asked at last.

"Yes please," I said, although I was *not* sure any more. "We'll be safe. We'll stay close to the train."

"Well . . . I suppose I can watch you out of the window . . ."

"Oh, *would* you?" asked Daisy—laying it on rather thick, I thought. But my father smiled. It's frightening how good Daisy is at reading people.

Back we went to put on our sunhats and outside shoes, and then we were ready for our expedition. Of course, heads came popping out of compartments all along the corridor to see what was going on.

"Outside!" said Madame Melinda. "Surely not! It sounds most dangerous. There are dark energies all around us—I can feel them! Better to stay inside, surely." She wrung her plump little hands. I thought how hot she must be in her black dress—but perhaps mediums were above all that.

"The English and their fresh air!" exclaimed the Countess. "And you are going, Alexander?"

"Yes, Grandmother," he replied nervously.

"Will you be chaperoning?" asked the Countess, turning to Hetty.

"Yes, my lady," said Hetty, bobbing a curtsey.

"Well, then—keep a sharp eye on them, that's all I can say," said the Countess in a very carrying voice. "You know what young people are like!"

Alexander and I went crimson. I thought I should die of shame. Why must grown-ups always say these things? Daisy inspected a spot of dust on her collar, and did not react.

"Yes, my lady," said Hetty again. "I shan't let them out of my sight, my lady."

So out we trooped, into the light summer air. The sun felt very surprising against my skin. I turned my head as we walked past Mr. Daunt's compartment and saw him glowering out at us. He must still be cross about what we had seen. Mr. Daunt, I thought, really was a very unpleasant man.

II

"What is it?" I whispered to Alexander, as soon as we were out of the train. It had stopped in a flat grassy clearing in the middle of the woods—though the trees were lurking only twenty paces away on all sides. We were in a tunnel of brightness, but it would not take long to step out of the light and be swallowed up by the forest.

"I told you, *something's happened*," said Alexander. "Listen. I was in Grandmother's compartment just now, helping her to find some things, and I looked in a drawer I shouldn't have. Grandmother yelled at me, and I closed it—but before I did, I saw what was in there. It was the *necklace!*"

"The necklace?" said Daisy sharply.

"You know—Mrs. Daunt's. The one that Grandmother thinks is ours. And now I don't know what to do. Grandmother can't be the murderer—she says awful things sometimes, but that's just the way she is, she doesn't mean it. All the same, if she's managed to get it, she's obviously done something stupid, and I don't know how to help her. I've taken it out of her room—it's safe in my pocket—but I don't know what to do now. She's family, see—I can't just turn her in!"

Daisy froze, and so did I. For all that we were out in the warm European sun, I felt suddenly dragged back to Fallingford in the rain, and all the dreadful things that had happened there.

"See, Grandmother sometimes doesn't behave the way normal people do. I think she actually did whip people in Russia, and I know she really was royal."

"*So?*" said Daisy, still frozen.

"So she might not understand that she shouldn't have stolen the necklace. But I'm afraid that if I give it to Dr. Sandwich, he won't see that this has nothing to do with the murder."

"Are you sure it doesn't?" Daisy's chin was up and her eyes were flashing. "Just because someone's in your family—well, all criminals are part of someone's family, aren't they?"

Something jumped inside me. "What do you want us to do?" I asked.

"Help me prove she didn't do it," said Alexander. "*Please.* I'm consulting you as fellow detectives."

Robin Stevens

I looked at Daisy. Would she help? Or was it too much like remembering the past? There was a pause, and then:

"You must understand one thing. We don't help. You help us. And there is a pledge that we need you to make before we go any further. This is very important. Do you swear not to tell anyone about what we do? If you don't, we will hunt you down and inflict dreadful medieval tortures on you."

As a version of the official Detective Society pledge, it was chopped down and rather cruel. Daisy had clearly not quite forgiven Alexander for being a rival detective, as well as a boy.

"Um . . . " he said. "OK." Then he broke into a nervous grin.

"Excellent," said Daisy. "Now, tell us: did you find anything else in her room—any bloodstained clothes, for example?"

"No! No way! Look, she couldn't have done the murder."

"How do you know?" asked Daisy. "What is she like without her cane? Can she move about without it?"

"Oh yes," said Alexander. "Although she always tries to hide it, she's terribly spry. She can almost out-walk me. But that doesn't mean she did it! She doesn't know any magic tricks—she couldn't have managed to lock that door."

He sounded so certain, but I could not help frowning.

• • •

It was all very well to tell Alexander that we would help him—but what he said didn't really rule out his grandmother at all. On the contrary, he was making her seem even more suspicious. If the Countess could move quickly when she wanted to, she might have had time to kill Mrs. Daunt and escape—and we now knew that she had the necklace hidden in her room. And that made the case even odder. We had a bloody piece of fabric and incriminating documents from Mr. Strange's room, but now the necklace had been found in the Countess's. All three were good clues, but spread out like that, what did they mean? The evidence seemed to point to two people at once—and now that we had discovered a motive for Sarah, it seemed that any of our remaining suspects might have committed the crime.

III

Daisy led us toward the back of the train, along the line of compartments.

I wondered why she had chosen that route—and then, of course, I realized. She was on the track of possible clues—and by walking past the compartments, she would find anything that might have been dropped there. It was a long shot—surely the murderer would have thrown whatever it was out of the window moments after Mrs. Daunt screamed, which meant that it would be miles back down the track, and quite lost—but it was better than no chance at all.

I tipped my head back and felt the warm of the day. I did like being in the sun, and I did like knowing that the murderer was safely in the Orient Express behind us. But then I stumbled on the rough stones, and although I had wanted to be free of the train, I suddenly felt exposed, like a snail peeled out of its shell. I thought of the bomb that had exploded on the line ahead of us, and shivered. Nowhere in the world was *really* safe, was it? There were always things lurking, ready to throw your life off balance.

While we walked Alexander made polite, cheerful conversation about the scenery, and the weather, and Daisy's pretty hat—no truly English boy would have done it, but I was glad he was filling up the air: no one who heard us from the train would suspect that we were detecting. There were no awkward pauses and silences, and no shy moments. I even found myself replying, although I did not need to. Alexander was all right, whatever Daisy thought.

On we went, almost as far as the dining car—and there, trapped in the coupling between the carriages, fluttering in the breeze, was a splash of dark red.

For a moment I thought it was a bloodstain, and my fingers went cold—but of course it was not.

"Oh dear," said Daisy. "Someone's dropped their scarf out of the window." She reached gracefully across and unhooked it, dangling it from her fingertips. It ripped a little, then fanned out through her fingers—it was fine, silky material: a lady's scarf. "Does anyone recognize it?"

My heart was pounding. This was the clue we had been looking for—it must be! It was a plain dark red, but I could see that there were darker dashes and marks speckled across it. Was that blood?

Hetty had her worried face on again. I could tell that she knew the scarf was important, but could not decide

Robin Stevens

whether to be responsible and tell someone—or curious.

Alexander looked worried too. "I don't know . . . I don't think I've seen it on Grandmother."

"But might it be hers?" asked Daisy casually.

"No!" said Alexander. "Maybe. I can ask."

"It's fine stuff," said Hetty. "Pretty."

"Too pretty to be Sarah's?" asked Daisy.

Hetty frowned. "She'd never be able to afford anything like that, but—"

I heard what she did not want to say: *but* we knew that Sarah sometimes helped herself to Mrs. Daunt's things. What if this were one of them?

"Daisy, we ought to hand it in to Dr. Sandwich," Hetty pointed out.

"Oh, don't be silly," said Daisy. "He won't know what to do with it. He's a bumbler!"

"Miss Daisy," Hetty scolded.

"Anyway, they've already found the handkerchief that was used in the murder. It was in Mr. Strange's room, remember? There's no need to confuse things."

"*Miss Daisy!*" said Hetty again.

"I *will* give it in!" said Daisy. "Eventually. But let's wait a little. Please. Be a dear, Hetty."

"Oh," said Hetty, "well . . ." I could tell that she was thinking of Dr. Sandwich. "As long as you give it in eventually," she finished.

"But what is it doing *here?*" asked Daisy, and I understood the question she was trying to ask. Who had thrown it out of their compartment, and why? It was all very puzzling.

"It might have fallen out by mistake," said Alexander, looking upset. I understood. This was a new clue—and it had not ruled out the Countess at all. On the contrary, if it really *was* linked to the murder, it seemed to point to a woman rather than a man—either Sarah or the Countess, rather than Mr. Strange.

"So we're agreed," said Daisy. "We keep this our secret—for now."

We all nodded. I was full of nerves—and it only took a moment before I recognized the feeling I always get when a case begins to rush down into its conclusion. We were close—and getting closer—but could I hold onto all the separate pieces of the case until we reached the end?

"What do we do now?" I asked.

"Turn back, of course," said Daisy. "I want to see the other side of the train before we have to go inside again."

So round the cold stopped engine we went; it loomed above our heads like a great black cliff, so solid and stationary; I could hardly believe that at a moment's notice it could be fired up and set off down the track. Then we began walking along the carriage again, on the corridor side this time. It really was strange to see it from the outside, as if we were looking at its reflection. The windows were too high

Robin Stevens

up for me to be able to peep in properly, but I saw the heads of people drifting past, ghostly behind the glass.

And suddenly, there in front of us, tucked into the gap between our sleeping car and the dining car, we saw two figures. They were lurking close together, standing out of the sun, but all the same I recognized them at once. It was Mrs. Vitellius and Il Mysterioso. Her face, under the dramatic picture hat, was tilted upward, and he was hunched over her—exactly like a vampire.

Then he caught sight of us. He threw out his arm and Mrs. Vitellius staggered against him. I was sure he was about to do something dreadful to her—she must have been confronting him about his spying—and let out a yelp.

"UNHAND HER AT ONCE!" cried Daisy, rushing forward.

"What's Daisy doing?" asked Alexander.

"He's the spy!" I said frantically. "I mean, there's a spy on the train, and he's it!"

"Oh," said Alexander. "Right. YOU! LEAVE HER ALONE!" and he rushed forward too.

Mrs. Vitellius waved her arms. I thought she was warning us to run and save ourselves—until I heard what she was shouting. "Stop it!" she shrieked. "Stop—good heavens— DAISY!"

Il Mysterioso turned away from her and, quick as a wink, grabbed Daisy with one hand and Alexander with the other.

He must have been really strong—they both struggled, but seemed to make no headway at all.

"Children—stop!" said Mrs. Vitellius. "Good heavens, do you want the attendants after us?"

"But—Il Mysterioso—is the spy!" Daisy puffed.

I was in a panic. What should I do? How could I save everyone?

"Don't be an idiot, Daisy!" said Mrs. Vitellius. "He's no more the spy than I am. Oh, *stop* for a moment and let us explain!"

At first I was not sure that Daisy would obey. In fact, I was not even sure about obeying myself. Should we listen to Mrs. Vitellius? What if Il Mysterioso were forcing her to pretend that everything was all right? I stared at him, and he held his hands up, letting go of Daisy and Alexander.

"Listen to her," he said.

Daisy rubbed her shoulder, eyes narrowed.

"I suppose I shouldn't be surprised to find that you're still interfering," said Mrs. Vitellius. "Or that you've dragged more people into your schemes."

Hetty bobbed a curtsey, blushing, and Alexander said, "What's going on? Is he really a spy?"

"You can't ask a detective not to interfere!" said Daisy, eyes blazing. "Hazel and I and our assistants are doing our jobs, just like you, and I don't see that you have the right—"

"Daisy," said Mrs. Vitellius, "for all your many good

qualities, you are fourteen years old. The British government has not hired you."

"*Yet*," Daisy muttered to me.

"You cannot come blundering into the middle of an interview and—"

"So this is an interview? I thought you said he wasn't a spy!"

"I did," said Mrs. Vitellius. "And if you'll listen to me for one moment, I can explain. Mr. Zimmerman's story is quite a different one."

"Mr. Zimmerman?" I said, confused. "Who's that?"

"That is my real name," said Il Mysterioso, and he bowed to us all. "Pleased to make your acquaintance."

"German really is an important skill, the world being what it is today," said Mrs. Vitellius. "I recommend that both you girls learn it. If you had been able to read those documents, you could have solved the mystery of Mr. Zimmerman some time ago."

"But . . . we know what the papers were, don't we?" I asked, bewildered. "Birth certificates, forged ones. Or isn't that right?"

"No, that's perfectly right," said Mrs. Vitellius. "And that's why I am speaking to Mr. Zimmerman now. As soon as I saw them, I knew that he was not the spy I'm after. Those birth certificates *are* meant to confuse governments, certainly—but not the British government. You see, if you

Robin Stevens

happen to be Jewish, as Mr. Zimmerman is, and you live in many of the countries of Europe, you find yourself in a very difficult position at the moment. If you try to leave your country with your own identity papers, you will be stopped. But if you stay, you will be treated very badly indeed. Alas, short of going to war, which of course we all want to prevent, there is really nothing we can do to help the Jewish people. It is left to people like Mr. Zimmerman to step in—he carries forged identity papers across international borders and hands them to his Jewish friends, so they can escape."

"But . . . that's smuggling!" I exclaimed. "Isn't that wrong?"

"It is," said Il Mysterioso in his rumbling deep voice, "but in this instance, *not* smuggling would be worse. The Fascists in Europe are not well-disposed to people like me."

"Why can't you just bribe officials to let you cross the borders?" asked Daisy. "Aren't European policemen frightfully lax about things like that?"

"The officials in question hate Jews more than anything else," said Mrs. Vitellius. "And most Jews, like most people, do not have enough money to bribe anyone."

"Why would they hate the Jews?" asked Daisy. Her nose was scrunched up, and I could see that, to her, it was not logical. But of course, there are some things that Daisy will never see; things that I know. The way people look at me, and speak to me—I have to tell myself not to mind, and so when Mrs. Vitellius said what she said, about hating Jews, I understood.

Mrs. Vitellius stared at me, and I gritted my teeth and looked away. Sometimes I do not like it when people understand me.

"People do not like difference," Mrs. Vitellius went on. "*You* ought to know that, Daisy."

It was a reprimand, although a very gentle one.

"Mr. Zimmerman's . . . unfortunate incident with his new magic trick proved to me that he was not guilty of the murder of Mrs. Daunt," said Mrs. Vitellius. Il Mysterioso rubbed his beard awkwardly. He was obviously still dreadfully ashamed of what had happened. "And from what I saw of the documents that were found in his compartment, I guessed what he was really doing. But I needed to make sure, and so I made an excuse to take this walk with him, to ask him to confirm my thoughts."

"And you told him about what you do?"

"It was the only way to get him to trust me," said Mrs. Vitellius. "I'm sure you both understand."

I remembered the moment, at Fallingford, when we discovered who Miss Livedon really was. Had Il Mysterioso been as surprised as we had been? I peered up at him, and suddenly found that I was terribly embarrassed. Everything I had thought about him had simply been wrong. He was not wicked, or dangerous, or a murderer. Underneath his beard and his cloak and his frightening face he was a nice man who was only trying to help other people, just like we were.

"I'm sorry," I said to him.

"No she isn't," said Daisy. "We *have* to suspect everyone, otherwise it wouldn't be fair. We were only doing our jobs."

"The girls won't say anything about this," Mrs. Vitellius told him. "They're very good at keeping secrets—aren't you, girls?"

"We have been known to be," said Daisy. "For a good cause—which I suppose this is. Oh, all right then. And Alexander and Hetty won't say anything either."

She turned to Alexander and mouthed, *"Medieval tortures!"* at him.

"Of course I wouldn't!" said Alexander. "He's helping people. It's exactly what the Pinkertons would do."

"I won't say a word, madam, sir," said Hetty. "Cross my heart."

"The next time I'm in London I shall give you all tickets to my performance," said Il Mysterioso.

"*After* you've perfected your trick, do you mean?" asked Daisy, a little mischievously. "And will we get ices in the interval?"

For a moment Il Mysterioso looked as though he were about to say no. Then he unclenched his jaw and said, "Naturally."

"Have you ever been to America?" asked Alexander excitedly. "Did you know Houdini?"

"I travel all over the world," said Il Mysterioso. "New York is no exception—and yes, I met Harry." Alexander's eyes lit up, and even I was amazed. Fancy having been able to call the world's most famous magician by his first name! "Funny, that was where I met Madame Melinda, though she was calling herself Mrs. Fox then. Quite an astonishing act she put on—she truly had talent. Had the whole place spellbound. Pity she's gone into mediumship now, but I suppose it pays better."

"What did she do?" asked Alexander politely.

"Oh, a voice act, you know . . . Very impressive."

So we had been wrong about Madame Melinda being an actress! But this was even better. I giggled at the thought of her singing.

"Now," said Mrs. Vitellius, "we ought to get back to our carriage before we're missed. It really will begin to look odd if I spend any more time with you."

"Indeed," said Daisy blandly. "People might think you were our governess."

"Oh, heaven forbid," said Mrs. Vitellius. "My hats are much too nice."

And she turned and hurried off, stumbling rather on the loose stones in her high heels; the courteous Il Mysterioso offered her an arm back to the steps.

Robin Stevens

We walked behind her, and suddenly I felt rather deflated. We had been so wrong about Il Mysterioso!

"Oh, buck up, Watson," said Daisy cheerfully. "We'll get there. I'm sure we're on the right track."

"But it isn't Grandmother!" said Alexander. He looked horribly worried again, and I did not blame him. Daisy ought to be nicer to him, I thought—after all, she knew exactly how he must be feeling. But Daisy is not very good at noticing when she is like other people.

"It's a good thing neither of you blabbed to Mrs. Vitellius about the scarf we found," said Daisy. "We may have established a truce with her, but we are still rivals in this mystery. We must get to the truth before she does! Alexander, you must keep watch on Dr. Sandwich's investigation. Let us know if he does discover anything useful by mistake. Hazel and I will follow the clue of the scarf, and see if we can narrow down our suspect list again."

"OK," said Alexander. "I—I hope you do."

I wanted desperately to reassure him that we would prove his grandmother hadn't done it—but that would not have been good detective work. I knew by now never to make promises I wasn't sure I could keep. So I only smiled at him, and he smiled back; a half-smile not at all like his usual wide grin.

"Come along, the three of you," called Hetty. She was

next to the carriage door, waving at us—I think she wanted to get inside again.

"Coming, Hetty!" Daisy called. "All right?" she said to Alexander.

"All right," he replied. "Gosh, I've never worked with other detectives before."

"Well, *with* is—" Daisy began. I glared at her. "No, nor us," she went on smoothly, as though she had never meant to say anything else. "We'll see you at dinner. Come ready to hand over your information in the most cunning way possible."

Robin Stevens

When we got back to Maxwell's compartment, my father had a surprise for us. He had ordered a delicious afternoon spread. There was a plate of éclairs and lemon tarts, and a pot of tea. It's funny how my father has embraced so many English things—even drinking tea when the weather is hot. After a year and a half of English school, I have nearly come to terms with it, but it still surprises me sometimes.

"Did you enjoy your walk?" he asked, smiling at us.

"Yes, thank you, Mr. Wong," said Daisy prettily.

"I have good news," he told us. "I have done all the work I can until we get to Belgrade, and so I shall be able to spend time with you again. I know I've been dreadfully remiss this holiday—not much fun for you, is it, having to amuse yourselves? And after I promised to show you Europe—"

"But we *are* seeing Europe," I said, thinking of the policemen, and the bomb, and Il Mysterioso's secret identity, and the unknown spy (who *was* it?) still waiting to hand over the papers in Belgrade.

"This is *not* the real Europe," said my father firmly. "Europe is history, and culture, and beauty."

Daisy stared at him, and I knew she was marvelling at how blind grown-ups can be sometimes. But I felt very defensive about my father. He did not understand, but that was not his fault. For once, it was up to me to look after him.

"We could solve some of the puzzles in our books," I said, and was rewarded when he smiled at me.

The three of us sat together and worked at crossword clues. It was oddly peaceful, and although I thought I should feel frustrated, I found myself enjoying it. It was good to be with my father, playing the sort of logic games that we used to in his study in Hong Kong, before I went away to school. I could tell that Daisy was frightfully bored, of course, but she disguised it well, and even pretended to get a few questions wrong, so that my father could be proud that I was cleverer than her.

At last the tea was finished, and all the éclairs and tarts had been quite eaten up. I felt hot and full, and very sleepy.

"Why don't you go back to your compartment and rest?" asked my father, noticing my eyes begin to droop.

"Oh, smashing idea," said Daisy, yawning daintily behind her hand. "I simply can't seem to *think* any more."

She was so convincing that I quite believed her—until

Robin Stevens

we got out into the corridor, where she turned right and stopped outside the Countess's door.

Jocelyn was back at his post, the room searches over. I smiled at him politely, and tried to look as though I was not at all worried about what Daisy was planning.

I could hear scuffling inside the Countess's compartment— bumps and scrabbles, which stopped the moment Daisy knocked on the door. There was a pause, and then the Countess opened the door. She looked flushed, little spots of color on her thin cheeks. Behind her I could see clothes and bottles of perfume and pots of face cream all flung about the floor—she must be searching for something, and I knew exactly what it was. She had discovered that the necklace was gone. I saw one other thing too—her cane was leaning against the far wall. The Countess had been searching her room without it; she was indeed more spry than she let on.

"Hello, my lady," said Daisy, bobbing a curtsey. "We're so terribly sorry to disturb you, but Hazel and I have just found a scarf, and we wondered if it might belong to you. It's a red one—terribly pretty—"

"It is certainly not mine," the Countess interrupted. "I don't wear red. It brings back too many dreadful memories. Those Soviet barbarians—they called themselves Russians, but no true Russian would behave as they did!" She seemed ready to launch into her favorite topic once more.

"Oh dear," said Daisy politely, "how terrible. Many

apologies for having disturbed you. We'll leave you now."

"Indeed," said the Countess. "You have excellent manners, young lady. Not like *some* young people these days. If there must be a new generation, I suppose it is a good thing that children like you are a part of it." And she shut the door on us.

Daisy made wide eyes at me. I was not sure what to think. The Countess had sounded certain about the scarf—and not at all afraid or worried—but then again, she was such a fierce person that she would be able to bluff.

Daisy was off again, heading for our compartment—but of course she went on to the door *next* to ours and knocked on Sarah and Hetty's door. Hetty opened it.

"Is Sarah there?" asked Daisy.

"What do they want?" called Sarah behind her.

"We've found a scarf!" said Daisy—before Hetty had the chance to shoo us away, as I could see she wanted to. "It's red silk. Is it yours?"

Sarah popped her head round the door, and her face, unlike the Countess's, did look worried.

"None of your business," she snapped, and I could tell that this time her fierceness was put on. "Go away."

"We were only trying to help. You oughtn't to be so rude. What would Mr. Daunt say?" asked Daisy.

"He'd say that you shouldn't be annoying me," said Sarah. "I may only be a maid now, but just you wait a few months and you'll see who's the grand lady *then*."

"Oh!" I said, before I could stop myself. Hetty's mouth was an O of surprise as well, and I saw a glint of excitement in Daisy's eyes—though of course she was pretending to be quite offended. It sounded very much as though Sarah was expecting something concrete from Mr. Daunt. But did she really think he would marry her? Servants didn't marry their masters; it was terribly shocking—but, then again, Mr. Daunt *had* been kissing her. It was only then that I realized how extremely odd that was. And so soon after Mrs. Daunt's death!

"Perhaps you ought to go to your compartment, girls," said Hetty, making a face at us. "It'll be time to dress for dinner soon."

"Yes, Hetty," said Daisy obediently. "Come along, Hazel."

"So," she whispered, as soon as we were back in our compartment with the door closed behind us. "Detective Society meeting, I think. It's long overdue. Yes?"

"Yes," I said, getting out this casebook.

"Excellent. All right. Present—well, you know all that. Now, to the clues. What have we just discovered?"

"That Sarah thinks she's going to marry Mr. Daunt," I said. "And that she and the Countess won't tell us whether the scarf we found is theirs or not. I don't think we should believe either of them when they say it isn't."

"Mmm," said Daisy. "I quite agree. Both of them are

untrustworthy—did you see the Countess without her cane?"

"Yes!" I said. "So we know that she might have been able to move quite quickly after the murder."

"That scarf, though . . ." Daisy went on. "It's odd. Now we've got that *and* the handkerchief from Mr. Strange's room. They're both bloody, so which did the murderer use to cover their clothes? If it was both, why only get rid of one?"

"I don't know!" I said. "There are *too many* clues, aren't there?"

I had meant it as a sort of joke, but Daisy's eyes suddenly went wide.

"Hazel!" she said. "Oh! I've just had a most interesting thought! We agree, don't we, that this murder was planned in advance—it didn't just happen." I nodded.

"So, if you were planning a murder, wouldn't you try to shift suspicion away from you, onto someone else?"

I nodded again, suddenly understanding where she was going.

"And part of that would be to drop *false* clues, wouldn't it? So we must assume that at least some of the things we've found were *meant to be discovered*. They're not real, they're only red herrings. So, how are we to know which is which? Well, in all my books it says that the planned murders are the ones where the murderer is most likely to slip on

242   *Robin Stevens*

some little thing that they couldn't possibly have foreseen. Therefore all we must do is work out what those unforeseen things were. Certain events have happened that *can't* have anything to do with the murder, and if we consider those, then we begin to see all the places where the murderer's clever planning went wrong."

"What things?" I asked.

"The bomb," said Daisy at once. "Even the very cleverest murderer in the universe couldn't have known that rebels would plant a bomb on the line ahead of us. They would have known that the train would probably be stopped by someone panicking and pulling the emergency cord when the murder was discovered, but we ought to have been on our way again almost immediately. After all, if you have a body on a train the first thing you want to do is get it to a place where the police can look at it, and that's Belgrade. So us still sitting here . . . that's a flaw in the plan. Which means that the scarf we just found . . ."

". . . oughtn't to have been found at all!" I finished. "It was meant to be lost in the woods somewhere, not caught on the coupling for us to find while the train was stopped. Oh, I see! So we were *supposed* to believe that the stained handkerchief Dr. Sandwich found in Mr. Strange's room was what the murderer used to cover themselves."

Daisy nodded. "Whether it was planted by the killer because it was supposed to lead the police to Mr. Strange, or whether it was a cunning double bluff set up by Mr. Strange himself, we don't yet know—but we must consider *that* as the planted clue, and the scarf we found this afternoon as the real one; the one the murderer never meant us to find."

I had to admit, it was one of Daisy's cleverer moments.

"What about the other clues?" I asked. "The knife?"

"The knife must have been planted as well," said Daisy. "It was wiped clean of prints, remember? Alexander told us so. If the murderer had enough time to wipe it after they used it to kill Mrs. Daunt, they had enough time to dispose of it too—yet they didn't. Why leave it with the body unless that was all part of the plan?"

"That's a clue that leads to Mr. Strange as well," I pointed out. "We all saw him carrying it about before the murder, didn't we? So when we saw the knife next to Mrs. Daunt . . ."

". . . we were bound to think of him at once," said Daisy, nodding again.

My heart was racing. Suddenly a pattern was building up—the two planted clues, so obviously implicating Mr. Strange. Had we stumbled on something important? But then I remembered . . .

"The necklace!" I said glumly. "That doesn't point to Mr. Strange at all, does it? It was in the Countess's compartment."

"I've been thinking about that," said Daisy. "We can't tell whether that is a planted clue or a mistake. Yes, it's terribly suspicious, but we know, because Alexander said, that the Countess is the sort of person who simply doesn't care about the law. Whether or not she is the murderer, she wanted that necklace—which means that there are three options. First, she is the murderer, and she simply couldn't imagine that she'd need to hide the necklace properly once she'd made the other clues point to Mr. Strange. Two, she is not the murderer, but the real murderer knew that she would be an excellent second suspect, if Mr. Strange was ruled out for some reason. And third—"

"Third, the necklace was planted in Mr. Strange's room by the murderer along with the other false clues, but the Countess went hunting for it, and pinched it from there while the interviews were going on!" I said. "After all, the compartments weren't locked, and Jocelyn wasn't guarding the corridor then either, because he was in the dining car. Anyone could have gone to his compartment without being noticed."

"Exactly!" said Daisy. We looked at each other, terribly excited. "So if we take away the clue of the necklace, what we're left with is this: the *planted* clues definitely lead back to Mr. Strange. He's Mrs. Daunt's brother and he needs money, which we know he'll get from her will. He really is the *perfect* scapegoat."

"So if we're sure they were planted, then Mr. Strange has to have been framed!" I said.

Daisy nodded. "And framed very well, considering he's

locked away at the moment, under guard. Oh, Hazel, well done to us! We've gone and ruled out a *most* important suspect! We're down to . . . two—Sarah and the Countess—and either of them could have done it. All we have to do is work out which."

"And *how* they did it . . ." I said slowly. Daisy frowned at me.

"Think about the knife," I explained. "We know that the murderer wiped it—but how was there time? The Countess might be able to move without her cane, and Sarah might be quick on her feet, but Mrs. Daunt screamed as her throat was cut. How could either of them have had time after that to steal her necklace, wipe the knife, lock the main door, set up the trick with the connecting door, and leave through Mr. Daunt's compartment, taking the scarf on the way, and hiding it and the necklace? All those things must have happened—we know they did—but how? And why didn't anyone see the Countess or Sarah coming out of Mr. Daunt's compartment?" The questions kept on tumbling out of me. I suddenly saw what a tangle everything was in. "Nothing makes sense!"

"It doesn't yet," said Daisy, "but it will. I still say that we'll be able to clear up this murder before tomorrow!" I couldn't agree with her. Something was wrong—terribly wrong—with our deductions.

"All we need to do is re-create the crime," Daisy went

Robin Stevens

on. "Just as I said earlier. We've been guessing about timings, haven't we? Let's find out for sure. You have to be Mrs. Daunt."

I sighed. Some things never change.

Daisy went to stand by the door, pushing the bolt home. "All right," she said. "As soon as I touch you, begin timing with your watch."

I took out my wristwatch, and looked at the second hand. Daisy stepped toward me, and as she reached out her hand I shivered. But all she did was draw it across my throat in a sharp movement. I opened my mouth, in a pretend scream, and began to count. Daisy pulled at my neck, as if she were unclasping a necklace (fifteen seconds). She stepped back, brushed something off her front (twenty seconds), and then used it to wipe something in her hands. She made a dropping motion—the knife—and hissed, "On the floor!"

I lay down on the carpet (twenty-five seconds) and watched her step over towards the connecting door, fiddling with it (thirty seconds), pretending to push it open (thirty-five seconds) and then closed again (forty seconds). She mimed stepping through it (forty-five seconds) and then turned to me and asked, "How long?"

"Forty-five seconds," I said, propping myself up on my elbows. "At least. Daisy—how can it be? We must have made a mistake. It only took us a few seconds to reach the corridor, and I remember Sarah and the Countess were already there!"

Daisy frowned. "But it *must* have happened," she said. "We know it did."

"I know!" I said, frustrated. "Oh—perhaps we'll find out more this evening. What do you think Dr. Sandwich is thinking, letting Madame Melinda hold the séance?"

"He doesn't know what he thinks," Daisy said. "He has no logic or method. He's an infernal bungler and he is confusing everything. However, even the world's greatest bungler may do something useful by mistake, and I think this séance *will* be useful to us. We must just watch Sarah and the Countess—will they try to direct proceedings toward Mr. Strange's guilt? Will they 'remember' something that isn't possible? One of them *has* to be guilty."

"I *know* what we're looking for, Daisy," I said—a bit crossly perhaps, because I was trying not to worry about what we had just discovered in our re-creation. I have been detecting for just as long as Daisy, and if I did not know how to watch suspects by now, I would not be a worthy vice president at all.

"I never said you didn't," said Daisy, holding her hands up. "Goodness, Hazel, you have got forceful this holiday."

I turned away from her angrily and began to write up everything that had happened, but I felt as if I was only going in circles around the problem. How would we ever

Robin Stevens

move forward? Both Sarah and the Countess might have done it, but there was nothing to choose between them; no way of knowing which of them we should point at and say, *It was you!* What if we never understood what had happened—and what if, when we arrived at Belgrade, the police believed all the murderer's red herrings, and arrested Mr. Strange officially? He would never escape once he had been arrested, even though he'd protested that he would. Even though I did not particularly like Mr. Strange, everything in me knew that it was wrong for an innocent person to be punished for something he did not do. It was not justice and that was the point of being a detective, wasn't it? To make sure that justice was done.

VI

At dinner Madame Melinda talked rather a lot about spirit energy, and Mr. Daunt took the bait. They had another of their furious arguments— it was absolutely clear that they despised each other, and both blamed the other for Mrs. Daunt's death. The rest of the passengers tried to pretend that they weren't listening.

After we had finished we were sent back to our compartments. When we returned to the dining car, it had a very different atmosphere. The curtains were drawn, and the candles were just little soft pulses, like red hearts. The electric wall lamps had been turned off—Madame Melinda explained that bright light interfered with the vibrations from the spirits, and I felt Daisy's silent huff of amusement against my hair.

"I've gotten these!" Alexander whispered to us as we all filed in. "Papers from Mr. Strange's compartment—there were lots. No one noticed me taking them!" He was so proud of himself that my heart sank. He was not to know that we had narrowed down our suspects again, and proved that Mr. Strange could not be one of them. These papers must be just notes for his new crime novel.

"We don't have much new," I whispered back, feeling dreadful, as Daisy folded them away in her little bag. "No one's claiming the scarf."

We all sat down in a slightly awkward circle, arranged around two tables pushed together, so we had to stretch out our hands across the white tablecloths. I looked at them all clasped together—my hand in Daisy's on one side (rather loosely, to show that although we were Detective Society forever, I had not quite forgiven her for her earlier comments), and my father's on the other. I had thought my father would refuse to allow us to take part, but he had looked at me very searchingly over his glasses and said, "If it is going to happen, then in the spirit of scientific inquiry we ought to watch it. It is important to know about the things that go on in the world."

I thought then that there were many more things going on in the world—and in our train carriage—than he knew. He might be good at business, but this holiday he had not been so good at seeing what Daisy and I were up to. Then I felt guilty. He had been busy with work; the work he needed to do to look after me and my mother—and my two little half-sisters and *their* mother, my father's concubine—and all the people who made our wedding-cake house in Hong Kong run as smooth as silk. I felt full of remorse, so I stared at my father's rather square, short fingers, with their deep knuckles and clean nails, and felt very fond of them. Once this adventure was over, I told myself, I would be a good daughter again, the very best there could ever be.

But only when this was over. For now, there was a murderer to be caught, and Daisy and I could not stop until the thing was done.

I looked up again, and around at the dim room. Beyond Daisy was Alexander, then the Countess, Mr. Daunt (looking very crossly at Madame Melinda), Mr. Strange (he had been let out of the guards' van, and Dr. Sandwich was hovering proprietorially behind him), Il Mysterioso (everyone else still giving him a wide berth), Mrs. Vitellius, Madame Melinda, Maxwell, and then my father again. Hetty and Sarah hovered at the edge of the room. Daisy and I had agreed that I should watch Sarah while she watched the Countess.

My hands tingled—with excitement, I reminded myself, not because of spirit energy. I very determinedly did not let myself get carried away by Madame Melinda's words. Auras, knockings, smells, and lights—they were all so many lies; magical red herrings to pull your eyes away from the real trick. This is what Daisy had told me firmly; and as was so often the case, Daisy was right.

Dr. Sandwich, though, was very enthusiastic. I could not

tell whether he truly believed that Madame Melinda would be able to call back Mrs. Daunt's spirit—but he certainly wanted to see her try.

Madame Melinda cleared her throat, and we all looked at her. "Good evening," she said, her rich deep voice like treacle. It seemed to ooze like treacle too, all the way into my head and down my spine. I shivered. I wasn't sure whether I liked it or not. Mr. Daunt snorted rudely, and Madame Melinda glared at him.

"We are here tonight, together, to commune with the spirits, and to call back from beyond the curtain the soul of our dear departed friend Georgiana Daunt. Spirits, we would know of you whether Georgiana now exists with you in joy—but we would also know of you whether she has darker memories, to help us discover the truth of her last few moments. Pitiful as they are, painful as they are to recall, we would ask you, spirits, to help us understand, to show us the way—spirits, are you there?"

As she said this, she raised her head, and half raised her arms, so that Mrs. Vitellius and Maxwell had to lift their hands too—and on around the circle the jolt went, each of us carried along with it without even meaning to be.

Then there was silence; a silence that buzzed with anticipation and made my hairs creep. Nothing would happen, I told myself—and then there was a hollow rap. It seemed to come from the tabletop itself, but I looked around at all the hands and saw them stretched out and touching, absolutely innocent.

Another rap, this time from—I could have sworn—the other side of the table; and then a perfect volley of them, so we all looked around in half-panic (though the grown-ups tried to hide their fear, and Daisy was only pretending). Off to the side, Sarah squealed, and I glanced through the dimness at her and Hetty. She did not look so much guilty as terrified.

"The spirits are here!" cried Madame Melinda, lifting her face up even farther—it seemed to glow in the dark-ness, and I blinked, for of course that could not be. "The spirits are here!" and then—and this made my skin crawl with horror—her mouth opened again, but the voice that came out was not Madame Melinda's at all. "We are here," she moaned, high and shrill. Then, deeper, "We are here," and, "We are HERE!" cried a voice so hard and heavily accented I could not tell where it came from.

"My spirit guides!" whispered Madame Melinda. "Welcome!"

I thought to myself that I would not welcome those voices anywhere, and gave up trying to hold Daisy's hand lightly.

"Spirits, we are here to contact one of the newest of your number, known in this sphere of existence as Georgiana Daunt. We would speak to her—is she there? Bring her forth!" Madame Melinda's head rolled, and the whites of her eyes shone. Strange noises came from her throat—groans and half-howls—and around us the knocking became a frenzy, until the whole air seemed to snap and shake.

Next to me, Daisy shivered. I squeezed her fingers tighter. That even Daisy should be afraid! She leaned her head against mine, trembling—and whispered two words: "Ouija board."

And of course, then I knew that Daisy was not frightened at all. She was not shivering. She was laughing. *Ouija board* meant, for us, the way Daisy had faked a ghostly presence to announce Miss Bell's murder to the school. Her trick with the Ouija board counter had been so clever that for five horrid minutes I had believed in the ghost. What Daisy was trying to tell me was that Madame Melinda was faking the knockings and spirit noises in exactly the same way that Daisy had faked Miss Bell. Nothing I was seeing or hearing was real; Daisy was reminding me of what had happened so that I should stop being afraid, and begin to be a detective. Again, I peered through the darkness at Sarah, and saw her shaking with terror.

"Spirits!" shrieked Madame Melinda, rolling her head from side to side like a spinning top coming to rest. "Speak!"

All at once, everything stopped. The carriage was bathed in another electric silence. And then a voice growled, "SHE IS HERE."

It did not seem to come from Madame Melinda's mouth, but from the empty air in the middle of our circle.

"She cannot speak for herself," the voice went on. "She is still too weak. She has not yet come into her full spirit powers. I, Baliostra, must translate."

Mr. Daunt snorted loudly.

"Baliostra!" muttered the Countess. "Ridiculous name." She clearly did not believe in the séance either—she did not seem afraid in the slightest.

Dr. Sandwich, however, looked excited. "What does she remember about the night of her death?" he asked. "What did she see?"

But it seemed that the spirits could not be hurried. Baliostra, speaking in very low growls (I worried rather about the state of Madame Melinda's throat), told us that Mrs. Daunt was at one with the light. She felt no more pain; only love toward those who loved her best. I suspected that this was a dig at Mr. Daunt. But then: "She wishes William to know that all is forgiven. The bonds of family love are strong—strong—and rise above earthly disagreements. But—oh!—when they are broken! That is the cruellest thing! When trust is betrayed—when family ties are disregarded . . ."

"Yes?" cried Dr. Sandwich, tightening his grip on Mr. Strange. "Go on!"

"In a place of light, she cannot speak of such dark

Robin Stevens

matters," said Baliostra—but what was *un*said was left hovering in the air. My heart began to beat faster. There were no spirits. There was no Baliostra. There was only Madame Melinda. So why was Madame Melinda, so full of anger at Mr. Daunt, still pointing the finger at Mr. Strange? Was it because she had been swayed by the planted clues, and really believed he was guilty?

"She merely remembers . . . a knock on her door. Unhappiness in her soul. A figure—a figure from her earliest life, one she knew so well . . . and words that have no place in the spirit realm. Oh! Something flashing in the dimness! Oh! Her jewels ripped from her neck!"

"And after . . . after she was called into the light?" asked Dr. Sandwich eagerly. "How did the murderer escape?"

"A cunning trick," moaned Baliostra. "Wicked—I cannot see—my eyes dazzle. The killer fled, to hide in plain sight . . . Oh, wickedness. Foul crime! *Oh!*"

And the carriage was pierced through with the most dreadful shriek. It filled our ears—it seemed to come from all around us, bouncing off the walls of the dining car and making it feel horridly small and claustrophobic. We all dropped hands in horror; the Countess exclaimed; Mr. Daunt jumped to his feet and Mr. Strange slumped backward in his chair, trembling with horror like a figure in a ghost story. Sarah was screaming. Was this her guilty conscience at last?

"Rather impressive," said Il Mysterioso. His eyes were glittering with professional interest. "Still up to her old tricks, I see."

Madame Melinda groaned and raised her head. "What happened?" she asked in a kitten-weak voice. "Did I see anything? Did I help?"

I was waiting for the Countess to mention the necklace—and so, quite obviously, was Alexander. He looked nervously at her, but all she said was, "This really is quite enough. I refuse to put up with this any longer. Take us to Belgrade *immediately*."

My stomach lurched. Was she silent now because she was finally feeling guilty for having stolen it—or because Madame Melinda had reminded her what had happened when she took it from Mrs. Daunt? Up to this point, I had not particularly cared about any of the suspects in this case, but helping Alexander had made me remember that, as always, real people were involved—people who mattered, people I liked.

"My lady, you need have no fear," said Dr. Sandwich grandly. "As soon as we receive word that it is safe to proceed, we will do so—and we will do so having cleared up this unpleasant business. I think I can say that my suspicions about the death of Mrs. Daunt have now been confirmed. The murderer is, without a doubt, Mr. Strange."

Robin Stevens

Part Six
The Detective Society Solves the Case

Mr. Strange slumped down in his chair even farther. His thin face looked more pinched than
ever, weak and unpleasant with terror, and he
put his hand to his neck as though shielding it.

"I didn't," he said. "Look here, *I didn't*—"

"There's no need to deny it any longer, Mr. Strange,"
said Dr. Sandwich, puffing out his chest in triumph. "We
know everything. Your books haven't been selling well,
have they? You needed money. You followed your sister,
Mrs. Daunt, onto this train—using the last of your dwin-
dling royalties, I assume—and begged her to help you. And
almost everyone agrees that they saw you walking up and
down the corridor brandishing a knife—"

"It's a *letter opener!*"

"A knife which you then pretended was stolen just before
dinner last night. Very opportune, I must say. Did you
believe you would get away with that? Then the murder.

You left your table at dinner and went to your sister's compartment. You covered your white shirtfront with this cloth"—like a rather second-rate magician Dr. Sandwich pulled the bloodstained handkerchief that had been found in Mr. Strange's luggage out of his pocket—"you took out your knife and you attacked her. Poor lady, she only had time for one scream before the end. Pulling the necklace from around her throat, you ran from the compartment, locking the connecting door behind you with a cunning trick."

"What trick?" snapped Mr. Strange, rallying slightly. "I'm not a magician—unlike *some* people on board!"

"There will be time enough to discover that later," said Dr. Sandwich, and I gritted my teeth at how very unrigorous he was being. "I'm sure a crime novelist would have no trouble concocting something. We shall get to the bottom of it, never fear. As I was saying, you dashed back to your own room, only to join us again in the corridor a few moments later."

Hearing that, I knew again that his explanation of how the murder happened could not be true. There was simply not enough time for any murderer to have done all that!

"Meanwhile, how do you explain that handkerchief? It was found in your luggage, after all. And those rather unpleasant stories we discovered—the ones about cutting a woman's throat—"

"Those are *stories*! I am a writer, an artist. I would never—Look here, man, it's fantasy. There's a vast difference between *writing* about a woman's throat being cut and actually *doing* it. The doing is far quicker, for one thing."

It was a very unfortunate joke. "DISGUSTING!" bellowed Mr. Daunt. "Take him away at once. Georgie's own brother!"

"Wicked, wicked man!" said Madame Melinda. "I'm only glad I helped bring him to justice."

"You?" said Mr. Daunt. "That penny trick of yours . . . *help?* That was a show, and a very bad one. It's the *evidence* that got him. We're in the twentieth century, not the sixteenth."

"We heard of his guilt from the lips of the spirits themselves, from dearest Georgie! How can you say such ignorant things! The ways of the spirits are the future; much is still to be revealed . . . Why, one day I believe that we shall live side by side, gleaning knowledge from each other equally."

While she was talking, Mr. Strange was led out of the room by two attendants; he was still protesting weakly.

"I wonder," said Il Mysterioso, "how Mr. Strange had time to lock that door behind him, and how he left no trace of his method of doing so? I am not sure even I could do it." Then, before Dr. Sandwich could say anything, he turned on his heel and, with a red swish of cloak, disappeared through the door. He certainly knew how to make an exit. I caught Daisy looking after him admiringly, and suspected that, next time she was taken to her dressmaker, she would develop a most mysterious interest in capes.

"He has a point," said Mrs. Vitellius into the silence. "How *did* he?"

"Mystery writers . . ." said Dr. Sandwich, waving her away. "They're cunning. He'll have come up with a clever way, and we'll get it out of him, never fear."

"And he ran the length of the corridor without being seen or heard afterward, to emerge from his compartment again!" Mrs. Vitellius went on. "Heavens, he *must* have been clever. I feel quite frightened to have been near him. Oh!"

"He ran very quickly, I'm sure," said Dr. Sandwich, evidently not interested in the discussion. "In his stocking feet. They do it in all the books."

And just like that, I knew for certain that Dr. Sandwich was wrong—not just about Mr. Strange, but about how the murder had been done. What he was saying . . . *it could not be*. And that meant . . . that meant that we were looking at everything wrong. But how? I could not think. It all seemed very real, but underneath it must be as faked as the séance.

I suddenly knew that I'd had a most important thought.

"Father," I said, trying to breathe calmly and hide my excitement, "can Daisy and I go to bed?"

There was no time. There simply was not enough of
it for the murder to work.

It was impossible, but we had believed it because
it had to be true. But what if . . . it was not true after all?

"What is it?" Daisy asked, as soon as we were back in our
compartment.

"Daisy—what if neither the Countess nor Sarah *did* do
it? What if we've been looking at this all wrong? What if it
wasn't just the locked door that was a trick? What if *everything* was?"

Hetty came in then, to help us get ready for bed, and we
had the most horrid pause. I was shivering with the effort of
pretending to be normal, and Hetty said, "Are you all right,
Miss Hazel? You can't really be cold!"

She turned out the light and closed the compartment
door, and quick as a flash there was a rapping on the bunk:
W-a-i-t.

O-K, I rapped back, though it almost hurt to agree. I closed my eyes and tried to calm my whirling brain. We waited until we heard Hetty going into her compartment next door, and then I heard a rattle—and almost shrieked when up onto my bed, like a serpent bursting out of the sea, came Daisy, eyes wild, hair flying.

"Hazel!" she breathed, so close that it made my nose tickle. "What *is* it?"

"I think—I think I've worked something out!" I whispered.

"Go down and see if it's safe to talk," hissed Daisy.

I clambered carefully down, crept over to the door and popped my head outside. It was a warm night, almost sticky, and the night-lights were on. The corridor was empty, although at the other end Jocelyn was sitting at his station, eyes drooping, his usually jolly face crumpled in a frown. He looked as unhappy with Dr. Sandwich's explanation as I was, but he seemed almost asleep. I closed our door again— it gave a tiny thump—and climbed back up the ladder.

Daisy had wriggled down to the foot of my bunk, sitting up very straight. She picked up the torch and flicked it under her chin, so that light fanned out over her face and the gold of her hair. She looked slightly mad, and utterly fascinating.

"What is it?" she repeated. "Oh, do hurry up, Hazel. I don't like waiting!"

I took a deep breath. "The timings don't make sense," I

said. "We've proved that. So we have to *listen* to ourselves. There simply isn't enough time for the murderer to have got out of Mrs. Daunt's room to safety. No one could have killed Mrs. Daunt the way we all think they did and got away with it."

"So?" asked Daisy.

"So," I said, "it must have been done another way entirely, at a different time. And if that's true, it means that everything—the scream, finding Mrs. Daunt's body—was faked. It was *all* a trick, not just the locked room!"

"Oh!" said Daisy, and I could tell that she had understood. "So you think the scream—"

"It can't have been the sound of Mrs. Daunt dying!" I said. "We can't prove it was, after all. We heard a scream, and we ran out into the corridor and saw Mrs. Daunt dead in her compartment. We assumed that Mrs. Daunt had screamed, and *then* died—but what if it was the other way round? It sounds impossible, because dead women don't scream—"

"Only they *do*, Watson," said Daisy, and she began to grin like a rattrap, "when Madame Melinda makes them."

I wanted to hug her. "Yes! That ghastly wailing noise at the end of the séance was *just* like the one we heard after dinner. No one realized what that must mean, because we were too busy thinking that it was a communication from the spirits. But of course, we know that Madame Melinda was controlling the séance, so if there was a scream, she made it."

"Goodness, Hazel, I never thought I'd hear you being skeptical about ghosts! But you're right, you're exactly right! *Why mightn't she have thrown her voice from her compartment into Mrs. Daunt's last night?* Their compartments are next to each other, after all, and we know from Mrs. Vitellius that she was in her compartment at exactly the moment when the scream happened. And didn't Il Mysterioso tell us earlier that she used to perform in music hall shows? We thought that he meant acting or singing, but what if he meant that she was a *ventriloquist?*"

Suddenly I saw a flaw. "But . . . Daisy, why would she? She liked Mrs. Daunt. Why would she kill her? And anyway, we know that she was in the dining car all evening; she left it with Mrs. Vitellius, and then she was in her compartment from that point until the moment the scream happened—so there was never any opportunity for her to actually commit the murder. Madame Melinda can't have killed her!"

"No, Hazel, you're not thinking quite widely enough. She can't have committed the murder—but *she must have been helping whoever did.* And she had a very good reason: Mrs. Daunt's will. Five thousand pounds, Hazel! It's enough to turn anyone's head—Oh, don't argue, *anyone unless they were as nice as you.*"

"But who was she helping?" I gasped.

"Mr. Daunt, of course," said Daisy. "Who else could it have been?"

Robin Stevens

III

There was a sudden shaking all around us. The compartment began to rock and judder, and the jug and glasses beside our basin made little jingles, over and over and over again. We were on the move!

I stared at Daisy in horror. If we were moving, we had a few hours at most before the train pulled in to Belgrade. Once again we were racing against time—we had to unravel the mystery as quickly as we could. Was Daisy right in what she said?

"W-wait," I said, stammering. "No—no, it can't be *him*. He hates Madame Melinda and he loved Mrs. Daunt! And he was at dinner the whole evening until the scream—"

Except there I stopped. Because Mr. Daunt *had* left the dining car, hadn't he? Yes, he had been in his seat at the moment of the scream, but earlier, just after he and Madame Melinda had argued and Mrs. Daunt had fled to her room, hadn't he gone to look in on her? He had come back a few minutes later shaking his head and asking Sarah to see what her mistress wanted, as if he had tried to get into his wife's compartment and been sent away—but how did we *know* that was what had happened? Sarah had gone to see Mrs. Daunt later as he had asked—we knew that—and we had also heard her tell Hetty that she had knocked on Mrs. Daunt's door and got no answer. Could it be that Mrs. Daunt had given no answer, not because she was cross, but because she was already dead?

Mr. Strange had *also* said that he had knocked on Mrs. Daunt's door and not heard anything, hadn't he? Again, we had thought that this was because Mrs. Daunt was cross with him, or, worse, that he was lying, and he *had* gone in and killed her—but what if he was speaking the truth too? What if Mrs. Daunt's double silence was not a coincidence, but a pattern? What if . . . what if . . . what if . . . ?

My brain was suddenly filled with *what ifs*, questions sizzling through it and turning my face hot with horror and amazement.

"But they hate each other," I whispered again.

Daisy looked at me pityingly. She was in control of the denouement once more.

"Partners in crime always pretend to hate each other," she said. "It's in all my books. The more two people argue in public, the more likely they are to be making plans in private. Unless they're not, of course. But this is not one of those times."

Robin Stevens

"So," I said, "if they did do it—"

"They did," said Daisy, "and here's why. First, Mrs. Daunt was rich. She had pots of money from her mother, and we saw her will—most of it was going to Mr. Daunt. And even though he behaved as though he was rich as well, we know that was down to Mrs. Daunt's money. She saved him when they married—it must have been *her* money he spent on the necklace, really. I know that he behaved as though he adored her when they were in public, but we heard them arguing when they thought they couldn't be heard, didn't we? She was so silly and spoiled—I'll bet he was sick of her. And that's why she was so upset all the time: because he was being cruel to her in private. When we saw Mr. Daunt kissing Sarah, we thought that it was a motive for her, but it's also really a motive for him. If he was in love with Sarah and he divorced Mrs. Daunt, he'd lose all her money—so why not kill his wife? That way he could keep her money and have Sarah as well.

"He and Madame Melinda must have banded together and decided to set the whole thing up, using Madame Melinda's skill at ventriloquism to create a murder that seemed impossible. That's why it all seemed like a play, Hazel! We thought so at the time, didn't we, only we didn't see what that could mean.

"Look, it's perfectly simple, really. They must have planned the crime before they boarded the train—but for it to work, they needed to wait for a moment when Jocelyn went through to the Calais–Athens coach. That happened at dinner, remember, and that was their signal. They staged an argument, knowing that it would upset Mrs. Daunt and send her running to her room. Then Mr. Daunt followed her, and *that's* when he killed her. He must have locked the main door behind him, protected his white shirtfront with that red scarf we found so as not to stain his shirt—the scarf could even have been Madame Melinda's; perhaps she lent it to him—and covered her mouth so she couldn't make a sound when he killed her. Then he took off her necklace, wiped the knife with the scarf, put it next to Mrs. Daunt and left the room through the connecting door into his compartment. Then he came back into the dining car as though nothing had happened."

"But how did he lock the connecting door from the other side?" I asked. "Do you think he used a bit of string or a shoelace, like when we tried it out on Maxwell's door?"

"He *didn't lock it at all*," said Daisy. "And *that's* the real reason why the murderers must be Mr. Daunt and Madame Melinda. We were being far too complex with our ideas. We were forcing things, to make the impossible work. But the truth is far simpler. It's that old logic puzzle: how can someone get out of a locked room? There are only three possible answers. First, they weren't in the locked room at all. We know that can't be true in this case, because Mrs. Daunt clearly didn't kill herself, so there had to be someone else in the room when she died. Second, they stayed hidden in the locked room until the rest of us arrived—we know that can't be true here either, because we all saw that there was no one in there when Mr. Daunt burst through the door. The compartment simply wasn't big enough to hide them. So, once you've eliminated those two as impossible, only one solution is left: that the compartment wasn't really locked. We saw Mr. Daunt break down the main door, and that made us all *think* that the whole room was locked—but remember how he went running into his compartment and came back out saying the connecting door was locked? We all simply believed him."

"But the connecting door was locked!" I said, remembering. "We heard Madame Melinda opening it—*Oh*."

"Exactly!" said Daisy. "She must have pushed the bolt to and fro to make it sound as if the door were being unlocked—but she *can't* have unlocked it because the murderer—Mr. Daunt—has to have left the room through it after he killed Mrs. Daunt. He didn't need to play about with string: he knew that his accomplice would make it appear to be locked later. Anyone not helping the murderer would have commented that the door wasn't locked, so the fact that Madame Melinda didn't mention that it wasn't proves that she must have been involved. And both of them shouting that the other did it afterward, when we knew that they couldn't have, just made them both look absolutely innocent. That must have been part of their plan.

"Then, later, one of them crept into Mr. Strange's compartment and hid the necklace and the handkerchief in his luggage. They weren't to know that the Countess would go hunting through the compartments for the necklace and steal it before the attendants could find it! They really did have an awful lot of rotten luck."

I suddenly remembered something else that made my skin crawl. "Daisy, when Madame Melinda opened the connecting door, she was holding a scarf in her hand. What if . . ."

". . . it was what Mr. Daunt used; the scarf we found snagged between the carriages. They must have tried to get rid of it, just in case there was something on it that might lead the police back to them. If they had prepared it beforehand, they could be sure that the handkerchief they planted to frame Mr. Strange was quite clean of everything but Mrs. Daunt's blood. But . . . why didn't Mr. Daunt take the scarf with him when he left after killing Mrs. Daunt?" Daisy frowned.

"Could it have been just another mistake?" I asked. "What if Mr. Daunt dropped it in his haste to leave, and when Madame Melinda saw it, she had to hide it quickly? So she picked it up and threw it out of her compartment window as quickly as she could—but she didn't do it properly, and that's why it got snagged."

"Yes!" said Daisy. "She couldn't plant it in Mr. Strange's room with the other cloth and the necklace, could she, as it was a woman's scarf, and quite possibly hers? It wouldn't have been believable. Oh, very good, Watson! What a lovely little detail."

My heart was pounding. What we were saying . . . it was all so incredible. But for the first time since the murder, what we were saying sounded *true*. I could feel that we were on the right track at last—and the logical part of my brain agreed. All those details that had refused to add up before had slotted into place quite beautifully. Daisy's eyes met mine, and we glowed at each other.

And then our compartment door slammed open. In the soft light stood a dark, furious shape. We both gasped. My heart was pounding. We were trapped! There was nowhere to go. Had Mr. Daunt found us?

A moment later a part of me was almost wishing he had—because when the figure stepped forward, it was not Mr. Daunt at all, but my father, and I had never seen him look so furious.

"WONG FUNG YING!" he bellowed. "WHAT ARE YOU DOING?"

"Who's that?" whispered Daisy. "Who's he shouting at?"

"Me," I said miserably. "He's shouting at me."

I know that things are bad when my father uses my other name. He strode into our compartment, and I saw that behind him was Jocelyn, hovering rather uncomfortably. We clambered down from my bunk and stood before them nervously.

"Wong Fung Ying," said my father, deadly calm, "I asked Mr. Buri to let me know if he saw any suspicious movements around your room. I was doing this for your safety, but when he knocked on my door to say that he had seen you peeping out a few minutes ago, and I came to make sure that you were safe, I heard you . . . making the most ridiculous, fantastical assertions about two of your fellow passengers! Hazel, this is not polite or ladylike! And I told you that on this holiday I wanted you to be on your best behavior! I did, did I not?"

"Yes, Father," I said, my voice catching in my throat and having to be forced out through a lump as big as a toad.

"Oh, Mr. Wong!" said Daisy. "We were just talking. We were making up silly stories—"

"Silence," he snapped. "Hazel, what were you doing?" My head spun. It was no good pretending any more.

I had to tell my father the truth about what we had been doing—and show him that we had disobeyed him because we *had* to. If we did not speak out, Mr. Strange would be arrested for the murder, and tried, and found guilty.

It was just like the Easter holidays again—a nightmare moment. In order to save a life we had to be believed, but how could we prove what we knew, and how could we make my father believe us? I knew I had only a few very short moments' grace. I had to speak more carefully and cleverly than I had ever spoken before.

"We were investigating," I said quietly. "I'm sorry. We were. But . . . Father, we had to. We know who really murdered Mrs. Daunt. It wasn't Mr. Strange, it was Mr. Daunt and Madame Melinda, and we have to tell someone, because if we don't Mr. Strange will be arrested for a murder he didn't do. You've always told me . . . You told me that justice was important, and if Mr. Strange is accused of murder that won't be justice. It can't be wrong to find out the truth; not if it saves someone—that's why we went on with the investigation after you told us not to."

"Explain," said my father. "Explain why you would accuse

two people whom you had never met three days ago of the worst crime known to mankind."

"Because Dr. Sandwich was going wrong!" I said. "And—"

"Because they *did* it!" cried Daisy.

I elbowed her. Not hard; only enough to warn her to keep mum. If she kept on, she would ruin everything. She shot me a look, but did not say any more.

"We wouldn't have accused anyone until we were sure," I said, "but we *are* sure now. That was what we were talking about. None of the other suspects add up—none of them could have done it in the time. There simply *wasn't* time, if you believe that Mrs. Daunt was murdered when we heard that scream."

"Dr. Sandwich accused Mr. Strange because of the knife, and the bloodied cloth, and his poverty, Hazel," said my father sadly. "This is not your business. Anyway, you know Mr. Daunt couldn't have done it. We all saw him in the dining car."

"But the scream we heard was faked!" I said, clenching my fists. "By Madame Melinda! She threw her voice, just like she did in the séance, to make us think that we knew when Mrs. Daunt was murdered. But it really happened much earlier—when Mr. Daunt left the dining car after his wife. He killed her without her making any noise, locked the main door behind him, and then left through

Robin Stevens

the connecting door. That's how the murderer had time to escape without being seen. Those clues you mentioned—those are all nonsense; they were planted by Madame Melinda and Mr. Daunt. Daisy and I found the *real* scarf Mr. Daunt used to mop up the blood and clean the knife caught between the carriages this afternoon when we went outside for a walk."

My father paused. "Hazel," he said at last, "this all sounds like the worst kind of detective fiction. I don't like what I am hearing—I don't like my little girl getting mixed up in all this nonsense."

"But I'm *not* little!" I shouted. "I'm nearly fourteen, and I know what's true and what isn't. I'll swear on anything you like that Daisy and I aren't making this up—honor bright we aren't. I don't tell lies: *you* taught me not to, so you ought to know that I'm telling the truth."

My father clenched his jaw. I held my breath. I had never spoken to him that way, never—how would he react? I should be beaten for it, I knew.

"Send a telegram," I begged. "Once we get to Belgrade. You can find out about Madame Melinda's music-hall act—whether she really was a ventriloquist. And can't you look at Mrs. Daunt's will? We've seen it—it proves that Mr. Daunt and Madame Melinda both had a motive to kill Mrs. Daunt—for her money." As I said this, I realized how thin it sounded. Mrs. Daunt had left something to Mr. Strange as well—and that would only seem to prove *his* guilt the more.

"The scream," I said desperately. "Please . . . the scream. Didn't you hear it at the séance? It sounded exactly like the noise we heard last night, when Mrs. Daunt died. Isn't that too much of a coincidence? Don't you see? If it was Madame Melinda who screamed then, doesn't it follow that she could have screamed on the evening of the murder as well? She and Mr. Daunt are working together, we know they are. You just have to prove it. *Please!*"

It was a long speech for me, and I was amazed at myself. I was being almost Daisy-ish.

"I ought to consult Dr. Sandwich," said Jocelyn, frowning.

"Wait, Mr. Buri," said my father. "Is that advisable? Dr. Sandwich does seem very set on his present conclusion."

I had been looking down at my hands, defeated—but my head whipped up to stare at him. Beside me, Daisy squeezed my arm so hard I had to clench my teeth. Was he really saying . . . ?

"Is there perhaps a way to test this theory—carefully, of course, without letting it be generally known? If my daughter and Miss Wells are wrong, they will of course apologize to you and the Compagnie Internationale des Wagons-Lits most humbly, in writing, and be subject to some rather dreadful punishments—but I do know Hazel, and she is an honest girl. She would not make an accusation like this if she did not feel she had grounds for it."

Robin Stevens

I gasped. I knew that this was a sort of test—would I crack and weep, and admit that I had been lying? But of course I couldn't, because I wasn't. My father and I looked at each other in the dimness of the compartment, and somehow his face seemed new, although it was still as familiar as ever—I suppose I was only seeing him in a new way. I wonder if he was thinking the same about me.

"This is only a suggestion," said my father, "but could you perhaps pretend to arrest Madame Melinda? This scarf the girls found, and the faked scream—could that be enough? I do not suggest arresting Mr. Daunt, because he appears to have an excellent alibi, and he is also a very influential man. If he is innocent, you would be hearing about it for the next twenty years. But Madame Melinda—she is a safer bet all round, and if she thinks she is being accused of the murder, who knows what she might say?"

Jocelyn frowned again. He clearly found it all most irregular and worrying—but all the same I could see that he had been bothered by Dr. Sandwich's less scientific methods. He wiped his hand across his forehead and came to a decision.

"If these are your orders, sir . . ." he said.

"They are my orders," said my father, looking at me unblinkingly. "Arrest Madame Melinda."

In the sleeping corridor, the noise of Jocelyn's knock on Madame Melinda's cabin door was thunderingly loud.

Daisy and I waited almost in the doorway of our compartment, and my father stood next to us. The train swayed as it went round a corner, and my father's hand on my shoulder steadied me. I still wasn't quite sure whether he was angry with me or not—was he doing this to shame me, and prove to me that I was still a little girl after all?

I craned round to look at him, and found him staring down at me, a crinkle of worry on his forehead. My father is still taller than I am, and for a moment I really did feel small and young and hopelessly foolish next to him. But then Jocelyn knocked again, and Madame Melinda's door opened.

Daisy clutched my hand, and I took a deep breath. Whatever my father thought of me, things were happening, and it was our duty to watch them.

Madame Melinda popped her head out into the corridor. Her heavy make-up had been wiped clean, and her face looked quite naked, bald as an egg and undefined. I barely recognized her.

"What is it?" she said. "I'll have you know I was busy communing with the spirits in the realm of dreams. They were giving me a *most* important message that is now lost."

"Madame," said Jocelyn, "my apologies for waking you. Alas, I have an important question to put to you. Do you recognize this scarf?"

He brought up his hand and dangled the red—and red-stained—scarf that Daisy had given him in front of Madame Melinda.

I saw her face twitch. "Of course not," she said. I knew then, with absolute certainty, that she was lying.

"You are sure? It does look rather like one of yours," said Jocelyn, still apologetically.

"It certainly is not," said Madame Melinda, drawing herself up to her full height and sticking out her bosom imposingly. "I only wear black. Now, please leave me alone."

"Madame," said Jocelyn, and I was concerned. He seemed rather at a loss. "There is just one more thing I would like to ask you . . . Forgive me. Is it true that you have had experience in music halls?"

Madame Melinda gasped. It was an inrush of air so loud that we all heard it quite distinctly. "How DARE you?" she cried. "How dare you insinuate that I might *perform* on the *stage*? I am an artist, a sensitive, I would never—"

"But the séance . . . your ability is obvious, madame. The scream—it was the work of a truly professional ventriloquist."

"Not bad!" whispered Daisy, impressed. I quite agreed. Jocelyn sounded so appreciative that for one second—and one second only—Madame Melinda's guard dropped. But a second was all it took.

"My talent *was* unequalled," she said with satisfaction—and then there came a horrid pause.

"That casts a rather different light on things," said Jocelyn, in quite a changed tone. "I was hoping you would admit it. Taking into account the scarf—which I believe *is* yours—and your vocal abilities, I believe that there is enough evidence to place you under arrest for the murder of Mrs. Georgiana Daunt."

"What nonsense!" cried Madame Melinda. "I was in my room at the time of the murder! I was—"

"But, madame, if the scream we all heard was nothing more than your thrown voice, how are we to know the true time of the murder? You might have gone into Mrs. Daunt's room at any time that evening and killed her—is that not right?"

"No!" said Madame Melinda, her powerful voice reverberating along the corridor. "No! I did not murder dear

Robin Stevens

Georgiana—how dare you insinuate that I would ever do such a thing! I am innocent—I am *an innocent*. I am in touch with the spirit world, next to which this mortal coil is base and ignorant. How DARE you!"

Doors were opening up and down the corridor and heads were popping out. The Countess came darting out, immaculate in a beetle-green robe, sleeping gloves and her lacquered cane, and out came Mrs. Vitellius, pretending to blink and yawn in a gloriously racy red silk peignoir. Il Mysterioso appeared, wrapping himself in his cloak, and then Alexander, looking curious and rather dazed. And out too came Mr. Daunt. I found I was holding my breath.

"*You* stood to gain by Mrs. Daunt's death," said Jocelyn, warming to his theme. "And *you* provided the scream that confused us as to the time of her death. I dare say you played another music-hall trick on us with that locked door. Madame, unless you can prove that you did *not* commit the murder—"

"I did not kill Georgie!" shrieked Madame Melinda. She sounded quite beside herself, and threw up her hands theatrically. "I tell you I am innocent. I did not kill Georgiana . . . HE did!"

And she pointed, with a trembling finger, at Mr. Daunt.

I could have cheered. I wanted to jump up and down and hug Daisy. Instead I stayed still—and watched.

Mr. Daunt swung his great bull-like head round to look at Madame Melinda. He had gone very red—*puce* was the word, I thought happily. He was puce with rage.

"You . . . " he growled. "You . . . you—"

But Madame Melinda had clearly had quite enough. "It *was* you!" she shrieked at him. "I know it—I can prove it. I never killed her—my hands are clean; it was you who did it—you murdered your wife!"

"Because YOU told me to!" roared Mr. Daunt. Sarah gave a sort of strangled cry.

"It was YOUR idea!" he went on. "I've been following your wicked plan! I can prove it—I'm just the dupe!"

"Dupe, nothing!" cried Madame Melinda. "If *you* hadn't wanted to get rid of her to marry your *servant*, I would never have suggested it. I was acting on your orders. I've lied for you, I've cleared up your mistakes and it was *you* who held the knife. I'll tell everyone—it wasn't me, it wasn't me!"

There was chaos in the corridor. Sarah began to scream and sob. "It isn't true!" she shrieked. "It isn't!"

Mr. Daunt ignored her. "You stupid woman!" he shouted at Madame Melinda, and actually flailed out with his fists at her. Jocelyn had to dart between them, blowing his whistle to summon help. "You told me this would be foolproof!"

Down the corridor came a gaggle of yawning, confused attendants, and behind them was Dr. Sandwich. He looked bewildered, his robe only half on and his moustache fluffy.

"What's all this?" he cried. "Good Lord! What a commotion!"

"Mr. Daunt and Madame Melinda have just confessed to that foolish woman's murder," the Countess told him, with great satisfaction in her voice.

"Nonsense—Mr. Buri, what is all this?"

"Countess Demidovskoy is quite right," said Jocelyn, rather wearily. "They have both confessed. Gentlemen, if you would please release Mr. Strange from the guards' van and put these two in their place?"

"Mr. Buri, this is quite . . . What is going on? How could they *possibly* have done it?"

Dr. Sandwich was obviously struggling with this new information. For a moment I felt almost sorry for him. How embarrassing to be so wrong!

"Good Lord, man, they confessed!" said the Countess, rather gleefully. "It's as simple as that. We all heard them—didn't we, Alexander?"

"Yes, Grandmother," said Alexander, and he leaned back against the wall. Then he edged along toward us, as casually as he could; as soon as he was close enough he whispered, "Thank you! *Thank* you!"

I smiled at him. I was so glad, I realized; so glad that he did not have to worry about his grandmother any more. Daisy merely nodded, and looked away.

"You'll . . . put it back?" I breathed.

"Already done," whispered Alexander. "Won't they get a shock when they check Mrs. Daunt's room at Belgrade!"

I was impressed with him all over again. He must have been so terrified—and he had kept his head.

Alexander grinned irrepressibly. "I owe you," he said. "Have you looked at the papers I gave you yet? They're terribly funny." And with that, he wriggled away back to the Countess. I saw him whispering something to her, and her exclaiming, and then they both disappeared into her compartment.

Now Mr. Daunt was bellowing and Madame Melinda was shrieking as they were led away down the corridor. They were both accusing each other of the most dreadful things—Mr. Daunt blaming Madame Melinda for not getting rid of the scarf before the train stopped, Madame

Robin Stevens

Melinda shrieking at Mr. Daunt that he had not left the connecting door properly closed, so she had nearly fallen through as she pretended to unlock it.

"Hazel," said my father, "Miss Wells, I think you have seen enough. Back to your compartment, if you please, and try to get some sleep before Belgrade. And once we are there—why, you deserve anything you want as a reward."

"Anything?" asked Daisy. She nudged me, and I knew what I had to say.

"We don't want anything," I said. "Only . . . from now on, will you let us do what we like? We really can look after ourselves."

"That remains to be seen," said my father, "though you have certainly acquitted yourselves well here. I think I can give you a longer leash from now on. I always knew I had a clever daughter, but it pleases me when I discover just how clever she really is."

Back we went to our compartment, and his words rang in my ears like bells.

VII

Of course, we did not get to sleep. I was writing everything up in my casebook, and Daisy was doodling on scraps of paper, trying to fill in the gaps.

"Do you think they knew Mr. Strange would be on the train?" she asked. "Or perhaps they had planned to frame Il Mysterioso until Mr. Strange got on the train too . . . Think what a perfect scapegoat Il Mysterioso would have been: a magician who knew all about locked-door tricks!"

"What *is* in the papers Alexander gave us, by the way?" I asked, not really listening.

"Oh," said Daisy. "They *are* frightfully funny. They're horribly badly written! Lots of heaving chests and bloodstained nighties. What a dreadful writer he is. It's almost— *Hazel!*"

Her voice had changed, and I looked up at last.

Daisy was staring down at the paper on her lap, electrified. "I held one up to the light just now—and *look!*"

She raised it again and put it against her lamp, rather

dangerously close. I was worried it would singe. But as she did so, brilliant little pinpricks were picked out on its surface—a constellation of bright specks.

"That's odd," I said. "There are holes in it."

"And the holes," said Daisy, "correspond to *letters* in that rubbish he was writing. Look—there's one over this *b*, and this *a*, and this *t*—and here's another *t*, and an *l*, and an *e*, *s*, *h*, *i*, *p*—which spells—"

"Battleship!" I gasped. *"Daisy!"*

"And look! This says *secret*, and this *five thousand*—Hazel, I do believe that, quite by accident, we have solved the mystery of Mrs. Vitellius's spy!"

"It was Mr. Strange!" Suddenly it made sense—why he had been behaving so oddly; why he, just like Il Mysterioso, was so reluctant to let on what he had been doing the evening before; and why he could afford to be on the train. *That* was what he was doing to get money—spying for the Germans! We had cleared him of murder, but he had been guilty of something else the whole time. And to think that *Alexander* had given us the crucial evidence!

Daisy and I both leaped out of our beds and dashed out into the corridor. A blue-jacketed wagon-lit attendant was standing there, feet apart, on guard. He gazed at us rather ferociously.

"Excuse me," gasped Daisy, "but we absolutely must go and see Mrs. Vitellius immediately. We've been arguing for ages about what we should wear in Belgrade and she's the only one who can help us. *Please*."

"It is two in the morning, miss," he pointed out.

"Oh, I know!" said Daisy. "We have no time to waste! *Do* excuse us."

And she hammered on Mrs. Vitellius's door.

Mrs. Vitellius was not asleep either, though she pretended to be, stretching and yawning as she opened the compartment door. But I could see books open on her bed behind her, and after she let us in she stood up straighter, not sleepy at all.

"Well, girls," she said, sounding slightly rueful, "I must admit, you have done it again. I didn't like it, and I still don't, but it would be remiss of me not to offer my congratulations."

Daisy accepted them with a nod. Of course, she thought they were only her due.

"As I told you before," she said, "it is the most excellent luck for you that we were on this train. Not only did we discover the identity of the murderer—before you, I may add—but we have now uncovered the spy! It is—"

"Mr. Strange?" said Mrs. Vitellius. "Yes, indeed. Now that, I think, I knew before you. I should call our scores one all."

That took the wind out of Daisy's sails. "But how did you know?"

"I am a professional, Daisy. I can make deductions. If

it wasn't Il Mysterioso, there was really only one person who fitted the profile: a frequent traveler, someone in need of money, someone easily led, with a rather loose sense of personal loyalty," said Mrs. Vitellius. "I have been suspicious of him for a while. And his comments about being released—he must have hoped to get in contact with his German masters once we reached Belgrade. I put two and two together and got my man. Now I've put a signal out of my window, where my contact will see it. He will know to arrest Mr. Strange—but I do wish that I had found some of those papers he intends to hand over."

"Aha!" cried Daisy, buoyant again. "*We* have them!"

"Alexander gave them to us," I said, feeling I had to be honest, "though we were the ones who decoded them."

"Look—he's been hiding his spy notes on the bits of paper he's pretending to use to write his book. If you hold them up to the light, you'll see . . . those dots! They're code."

Mrs. Vitellius, frowning, held up the piece of paper. Then her serious face broke into a smile. "Daisy Wells," she exclaimed. "You've done it again."

"Hazel and I did it together," said Daisy—to my surprise. "But we did! You see, without Hazel, I would never be on this train in the first place, and so you would all have been deprived of my brilliance."

I grinned. It was an utterly Daisy-ish thing to say.

VIII

We reached Belgrade at seven in the morning, under wet gray clouds that made the dark gray stones of the city look deeply gloomy. I was sticky-eyed from tiredness, but all the same I was quite overwhelmed with excitement. Our detective work had paid off again—that was *three* real cases that the Detective Society had solved! Now no one could claim that we were not proper detectives, not even my father.

As soon as we pulled up in the echoing, smoky station, policemen swarmed around the train. They came rushing up the steps, muddying the lovely carpets with their boots and knocking against the beautiful wooden walls with the barrels of their guns.

"Just like our English clodhoppers," said Daisy, mock-sorrowfully.

Then on jumped one more policeman, raincoat flapping. The golden hair under his cap gleamed and there was the quirk of a smile on his handsome face. He looked down at us through his monocle, and his expression did not change at all, apart from one elegantly raised eyebrow. Daisy raised an eyebrow back. I tried not to grin. I had no idea how M had come here—but here he was.

The golden policeman turned to Mrs. Vitellius, who had come out of her compartment and was standing beside us. There was a brief moment when they stared at each other quite blankly, Mrs. Vitellius squaring her chin and the policeman raising his eyebrow again. "Fetch Mr. Strange," he barked to the two men behind him.

Then he said, in quite a different tone, "Mrs. Vitellius, I believe?"

"Indeed," she replied. "And who might you be—so English and so far from home?"

"Who I am is no concern of yours," said the policeman. "Although I could show you papers proving that, despite my accent, I am Serbian. But I have some news for you. Your husband, Mr. Vitellius, has made some . . . rather unwise investments, and is therefore no longer waiting for you in Istanbul. Instead, he is in this city, under arrest. Given the situation, I would ask you to accompany me to where he is being held."

"Good heavens," said Mrs. Vitellius, quite calmly. "How dreadful! At once, you say?"

"Immediately," said the golden policeman. "Although it

would be remiss of me if I did not allow you to collect your hats."

And he winked at her, just once.

Mr. Strange was heaved off the train, protesting, and five minutes later Mrs. Vitellius and the policeman left together, her hand on his escorting arm—and as he passed us his free hand brushed against Daisy's, just for a moment.

Afterwards, in our compartment, Daisy opened the letter he had given her.

Dear Detectives,

Jolly good show, and excellent work once again. I ought to punish you, of course, but I obviously have no control over you whatsoever—and besides, you seem to be doing perfectly well on your own. I am proud to never know what you will do next.

—M.

Daisy folded it up and put it in her little bag.

"*Now* will you tell me what your uncle does?" I asked, for what I had just seen seemed to confirm more of the school legends I had heard.

"Of course I won't," said Daisy. "Official secrets. Really, though, if I had to be related to anyone—I'm glad it's him.

"This whole business of the spy—how odd that it was going on at the same time as our murder! It's quite funny, really—all the things that are going on all the time. That's what makes murder so cluttered. If other people were as logical as me, every one of our cases would be solved in five seconds flat. What are you smiling at?"

"Nothing," I said, putting my arm through hers.

IX

M adame Melinda and Mr. Daunt were taken away by more police. Madame Melinda shrieked, and Mr. Daunt bellowed, but Jocelyn was more resolute than I could ever have imagined. He stood to one side, his face set, while the other passengers poked their heads out of the train windows and looked scandalized.

Off they went, in handcuffs, and there was peace.

But then I looked out of the window again—and caught one brief, smoky glance of Il Mysterioso, fading away down the platform, his cloak wrapped tightly around him and his papers, in their magic box, quite safe in the case he swung from one powerful arm. It was almost like one last magic trick: I blinked, and he was gone. I wondered about those people, the ones he was taking those papers to . . . What would it mean to them, that Il Mysterioso was still free? I could not imagine not being safe in my own home—and then I thought that perhaps I could. Here in the middle of Europe I could float, neither English nor Chinese, but I would always be going to somewhere, from somewhere, and where those places were mattered.

I turned back to our compartment—to Daisy, who was so good at pretending to fit in, but all the same was just as different as I was—and she smiled at me.

"Why the long face, Hazel?" she said. "You ought to be dreadfully pleased. After all, we solved a murder. Again! Although really I was the one who tumbled to the answer."

"I suppose you did," I said. For once, I decided, I would allow Daisy her triumph.

"Although you were helpful," she conceded. "Good at hiding under tables, and so on. Excellent Watsoning."

"Idiot," I said, making a face. "I'm not sure my father will ever forgive me, really."

"Yes he will," said Daisy. "He's ever so proud of you, I can tell. Lucky you, having a father who knows you like that."

For a moment I could not look at her.

"But I suppose it's back to holidaying properly now," said Daisy. "Hmm. I suppose I could holiday for a while."

"I don't know," I said, grinning. I thought of Alexander, and the Junior Pinkertons. Despite what Daisy said, I thought how nice it was to know that there were other detectives just like us. It made the world feel very wide, and very interesting. "We've still got almost a day before we reach Istanbul. *Anything* might happen."

Daisy's
Guide to the
Orient Express

O nce again, Hazel has asked me to explain some of the words she has used in the Case of the Great Train Murder. I had expected more of them to be about trains, but Hazel is not always very rigorous with her descriptions. Nevertheless, I shall do my best with what I have been given.

Blind—a trick. It is from a hunting word: hunters hide behind covers called blinds, so that the pheasants cannot see them until it is too late.

Brick—a good sort of person, someone who keeps important secrets without being asked and shares out any food they are given. Hetty is a brick.

Buck up—this is an order that means that you need to take hold of yourself and be firm. If you are not bucked up, you are weak and wobbling, and that, in a detective, will never do.

Charlatan—a lying sort of person who pretends to be something they are not for money.

Concubine—this is not at all an English word. It means a Chinese lady who is not a man's first wife, but is kept about his house.

Copper magnate—a magnate is a person who is rich from owning lots of businesses. A copper magnate simply means someone who has got very rich from owning copper mines.

Dorm—the building where girls sleep. You also have smaller dorm rooms inside it. When you are shrimps you sleep all together with all the other girls in your class, but as you become a bigger girl you are allowed to pick your dorm mates.

Eau de nil—this is a color, a sort of pale green.

Fire iron—what funny words Hazel has chosen! As everyone knows, this is something metal that you use to poke a fire.

Good egg—rather like a brick. This is a person who can always be trusted to do the correct thing.

Honor bright—a sacred promise. Once you have sworn to do something "honor bright," you must do it or no one will ever trust you again.

Housemistress—the woman who looks after our dorm and tells us to brush our hair and clean our faces. Our housemistress, Mrs. Strike, is always confiscating our goodies and then eating them herself, because she is a greedy pig.

Keep mum—stay quiet. In many detective situations it is crucial to keep mum.

Marquetry—a sort of shiny wood decoration that can be in the shape of flowers or birds. It is very pretty to look at, but otherwise useless.

Melusine—a water nymph from myth. She had a tail instead of legs, so if she had been put down in a corridor she would have crawled.

Mui jai—another Chinese word. This is a sort of woman servant in China who looks after a family. Hazel has one.

Pax—this word means "peace" in Latin. It is a way of asking someone to be your friend, at least for a while.

Peignoir—a sort of racy nightie for grown-ups.

Plus fours—golfing trousers that stop at your knees.

Shorthand—a way of writing. It is useful because it can be noted down as quickly as speech. I have tried to persuade Hazel to learn it, but so far she has been stubborn. After this case, though, I think she will see the point.

Shrimps—the smaller girls at Deepdean School.

Robin Stevens

Soviets—the Communist sort of Russians. They go about waving red banners and deposing tsars, and are generally not the sort of people you would like to meet.

Stenographer—a professional note-taker.

Stereoscope—this is a very clever toy that looks like binoculars, but when you put it to your eyes you see photographs. They are especially clever, though—they look as if they are absolutely real and jumping toward you, rather than just being flat and dull.

Take someone down a peg or two—this means teaching someone a lesson. If you are stuck up, you need taking down a peg or two. Hazel is wrong about me needing this sometimes—I am absolutely perfect, and do not need taking down at all.

Tesla machine—this is a very exciting electrical machine invented by a man called Mr. Tesla. It makes sparks come out of your hair, or at least, that's what I've heard.

Toilette—the word for putting on or taking off your make-up.

Tsar—the Russian word for king. In 1917 the nasty Soviets went mad and had a revolution: they stormed the Russian palace and killed the tsar and all his family, even the littlest ones. The Soviets were not good eggs.

Turning down—the phrase for tidying a room and making sure the blankets and linens are all nice. On a train, this means folding down the bunks into beds each evening.

View-halloo—a special hunting word that can also be used when you are after a criminal, and about to catch them.

Wagon-lit—the French for "sleeping car."

Wizard—a slang word that means spiffing or excellent.

ACKNOWLEDGMENTS

Agatha Christie's *Murder on the Orient Express* has fascinated me since I first read it fifteen years ago. I love its characters, I love its neat, astonishingly clever denouement, and I've watched the 1974 Albert Finney film version twenty times at least. So, of course, it took my wise editor Natalie Doherty asking whether Hazel and Daisy could solve a murder on a train for it to occur to me that I could write my own tribute to it. My first thanks, therefore, have to go to her—for the original idea, and for all the work she has done to shape the story since.

As part of the research for *First Class Murder*, I decided that I needed to experience as much of the Orient Express as possible (minus the murder). So on October 4, 2014, I took a lunch excursion in an original British Pullman train, laid out just as the Orient Express dining cars of the 1930s would have been. Many thanks to the staff I met on my journey—especially Jeff Monks for answering all my strange questions (as a result of our conversation, I regretfully removed ice cream from my menu), and Arthur for looking after me so well. The meal Daisy and Hazel eat on the evening of the murder matches the lunch I was given—apart from the crêpes Suzette, for which I used my imagination.

Hazel's Chinese name appears in this book for the first time— it is Wong Fung Ying, or 皇鳳英 (Wong appears first here because

Chinese convention is to put a person's family name before their given name.) Literally translated, "Wong Fung Ying" means "Royal Phoenix Brave" or "Royal Phoenix England." My friend Scarlett Fu did incredible research into Hong Kong naming conventions of the 1920s to come up with this name—many, many thanks to her for the time she took. She gave me several auspicious options, and I could not resist this one. It seemed to me that Mr. Wong, with his fondness for England and his belief in the importance of knowledge, would have given his daughter a name that was not just beautiful, but extremely strong.

As always, this book could not exist without the help of many fantastic people. Thank you to my agent, Gemma Cooper, who is quite simply one of the best people I have ever met. She has never come across a problem she could not defeat, and I am proud to be her client and a client of the Bent Agency. Thank you to early readers Kathie Booth Stevens and Melinda Salisbury (I took the liberty of borrowing Melinda's first name for this book, though not, I promise, her character). Thank you to Harriet Reuter Hapgood for the excellent title, and to all of Team Cooper for their help, support, and judicious provision of wine. Thank you to everyone at Simon and Schuster Books for Young Readers, in the editorial, PR, marketing, design and sales teams, who have helped bring Hazel and Daisy to the USA, especially my editorial team Kristin Ostby and Mekisha Telfer, my cover illustrator Elizabeth Baddeley, and Felicity, who I hope will read this book one day. Thank you also to all the other people who have supported me through this process: my friends, my family and the people I worked with at Egmont while I was writing this book.

And finally, thank you to *you*—to each of the booksellers and bloggers and readers who have supported this series in the most incredible way. Thank you for every recommendation, every reader email, every tweet, every review, every event and every bookshop display. I have been completely astonished by the way every one of you has personally supported my heroines and their stories. Meeting and speaking to my readers is one of the most special things about being an author—if I could, I would give each one of you your own Detective Society badge.

Long may the adventures continue.

Robin Stevens

April 2016

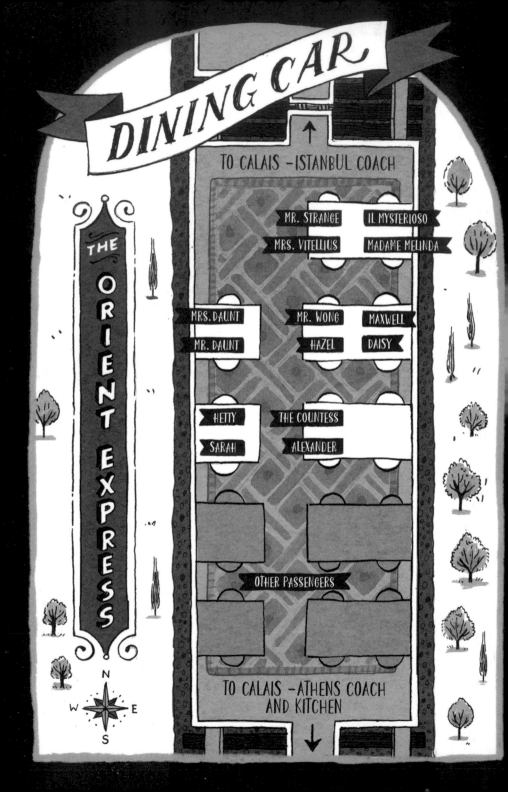